V.8

Other Bc

AN INSPECTOR DE SILVA MYSTERY

TAKEN
IN NUALA

HARRIET STEEL

MYS
STEEL

Author's Note and Acknowledgements

Welcome to the eighth book in my Inspector de Silva mystery series. Like the earlier ones, this is a self-contained story but, wearing my reader's hat, I usually find that my enjoyment of a series is deepened by reading the books in order and getting to know major characters well. With that in mind, I have included thumbnail sketches of those featuring here who took a major part in previous stories. I have also reprinted this introduction, with apologies to those who have already read it.

Several years ago, I had the great good fortune to visit the island of Sri Lanka, the former Ceylon. I fell in love with the country straight away, awed by its tremendous natural beauty and the charm and friendliness of its people who seem to have recovered extraordinarily well from the tragic civil war between the two main ethnic groups, the Sinhalese and the Tamils. I had been planning to write a detective series for some time and when I came home, I decided to set it in Ceylon in the 1930s, a time when British Colonial rule created interesting contrasts, and sometimes conflicts, with traditional culture. Thus, Inspector Shanti de Silva and his friends were born.

I owe many thanks to everyone who helped with this book. My editor, John Hudspith, was, as usual, invaluable and Jane Dixon Smith designed another excellent cover for me, as well as doing the elegant layout. Praise from the many readers who told me that they enjoyed the previous books in this series and wanted to know what Inspector de Silva and his friends got up to next encouraged me to keep going. Above all, heartfelt thanks go to my husband, Roger, without whose unfailing encouragement and support I might never have reached the end.

Apart from well-known historical figures, all characters in the book are fictitious. Nuala is also fictitious although loosely based on the hill town of Nuwara Eliya. Any mistakes are my own.

**Characters who appear regularly
in the Inspector de Silva Mysteries**

Inspector Shanti de Silva. He began his police career in
Ceylon's capital city, Colombo, but, in middle age, he married and accepted a promotion to inspector in charge of
the small force in the hill town of Nuala. Likes: a quiet
life with his beloved wife, his car, good food, his garden.
Dislikes: interference in his work by his British masters;
formal occasions.

Sergeant Prasanna. Nearly thirty and married with a
daughter. He's doing well in his job and starting to take
more responsibility. Likes: cricket and is exceptionally good
at it.

Constable Nadar. A few years younger than Prasanna. Dif-
fident at first, he's gaining in confidence. Married with two
boys. Likes: his food; making toys for his sons. Dislikes:
sleepless nights.

Jane de Silva. She came to Ceylon as a governess to a
wealthy colonial family and met and married de Silva a few
years later. A no-nonsense lady with a dry sense of humour.
Likes: detective novels, cinema, and dancing. Dislikes:
snobbishness.

Archie Clutterbuck. Assistant government agent in Nuala
and as such, responsible for administration and keeping law
and order in the area. Likes: his Labrador, Darcy; fishing;
hunting big game. Dislikes: being argued with; the heat.

Florence Clutterbuck. Archie's wife, a stout, forthright lady. Likes: being queen bee; organising other people. Dislikes: people who don't defer to her at all times.

William Petrie. Government agent for the Central Province and therefore Archie Clutterbuck's boss. A charming exterior hides a steely character. Likes: getting things done. Dislikes: inefficiency.

Lady Caroline Petrie. His wife and a titled lady in her own right. She is a charming and gentle person.

Doctor David Hebden. Doctor for the Nuala area. He travelled widely before ending up in Nuala. He's married to Emerald, but they have no children. Under his professional shell, he's rather shy. Likes: cricket. Dislikes: formality.

Emerald Hebden (née Watson). She arrived in Nuala with a touring British theatre company and decided to stay. She's a popular addition to local society. Her full story is told in *Offstage in Nuala*.

Charlie Frobisher. A junior member of staff in the Colonial Service. A personable young man who is tipped to do well. Likes: sport and climbing mountains.

CHAPTER 1

The Residence was lit up for a grand party. The classically proportioned house – the official home of the British assistant government agent in charge of Nuala and the Hill Country, Archie Clutterbuck and his wife Florence – was always an impressive sight, but that evening, touches of gaiety gave it a festive appearance. Red, white and blue bunting strung between the columns of the entrance portico swayed gently in the warm air. Strings of fairy lights glittered in the palm trees.

'It feels like Christmas,' remarked de Silva as he edged the Morris into a space between a green Hillman and a black Austin 7.

'Very pretty,' his wife Jane said from the passenger seat.

Safely parked, he turned off the engine and walked around the car to open the door for her. They paused to admire the charming picture that the Residence made, then, arm in arm, crossed the gravelled sweep. As they climbed the entrance portico's wide steps, the sound of conversation and laughter greeted them.

Inside, banks of greenery and flowers decorated the reception hall. The teak floor had been freshly polished for the occasion, and the air was perfumed with beeswax and the scent of flowers. Richly coloured silk hangings glowed on the walls, and they also displayed some finely carved wooden panels depicting a variety of scenes from Ceylonese folklore. Portraits of stern-faced colonial officers who had served in Nuala added a more sombre note. Chandeliers blazed and, in their dazzling light, Archie and Florence waited with smiles on their faces to greet their guests.

'Jane, dear!' trilled Florence when the de Silvas reached the head of the line. 'How nice you look. We're so glad you both could come.'

She gave Jane a peck on the cheek then smiled at de Silva. He bowed gravely. 'It's a great pleasure to be invited, ma'am.'

'I'm sure there will be lots of people you know here,' Florence went on. 'Lady Caroline and William Petrie have done us the honour of attending. They were asking after you, so you must be sure to pay your respects.'

That wouldn't be a hardship, thought de Silva. He and Jane both liked Petrie, the government agent based in Kandy, who was Archie's boss, and his wife, Lady Caroline. They hadn't met since that fateful cruise to Egypt, the resounding memory of which seemed, to de Silva, to be of him clinging on to a galloping camel. He couldn't help but smile.

'Pleasure to see you both,' boomed Archie. Spruced up in black evening attire, his jacket emblazoned with a row of medals, he already had beads of sweat on his forehead.

'Likewise, sir.' De Silva gestured to the queue behind them, saying to Clutterbuck. 'You have a great many guests tonight.'

'The more the merrier, eh?'

'And the more funds we raise for the orphanage,' added Florence. 'I'm determined to outdo last year's efforts.'

'I'm sure you will, ma'am.'

Florence wagged a finger at him and smiled. 'You must buy lots of raffle tickets, Inspector. We have some wonderful prizes.'

As they moved on towards the Residence's ballroom,

where guests were assembling for pre-dinner drinks, de Silva muttered to Jane under his breath. 'Florence is very affable tonight, but my goodness, raffle prizes! I remember last year. How many china cats and knitted tea cosies does one household need?'

Jane giggled. 'Hush, Florence might get to hear. You know how hard she works to make this party a success, and the orphanage is such a good cause.'

'I know it is.' He looked contrite. 'I suppose we can find room on the mantelpiece for one more ornament.'

'Perhaps we'll win the first prize.'

'A life-sized china elephant?'

'Don't be silly, dear. Florence has persuaded Archie to donate a case of his favourite whisky.'

'Now, *that* would be worth winning.'

In the ballroom, they both chose fresh mango juice from the tray of drinks a waiter offered. Many of the other guests had already arrived, and the room would have been too hot had not all the doors to the gardens been open. Luckily, mosquitoes were rarely troublesome in the Hill Country. De Silva noticed a piano and a collection of music stands on the raised dais to one side of the room and recalled that last year there had been dancing. He hoped he wasn't expected to lead Florence onto the floor. Dancing with his wife was a pleasure, but with Florence it was more likely to be an ordeal. Discombobulated by her eagle eye, he was bound to put numerous feet wrong.

Doctor Hebden and his wife, Emerald, squeezed through the throng to join them.

'How lovely to see you both,' said Emerald. 'Time's simply flown since we came back from our honeymoon; we've been so busy in the house. You simply must come and see the improvements when everything's finished.' She slipped her hand into the crook of her husband's arm. 'Mustn't they, darling?'

'Certainly they must. Although I'll admit straight away that I can't take any of the credit. That's all down to Emerald.'

'I look forward to seeing it,' said Jane, amused.

De Silva noticed David Hebden's cheerful expression as the ladies chatted on. He was glad that married life seemed to suit the local doctor so well. He'd always liked Hebden – an unassuming, thoroughly decent man, who'd often been a help to him in his police work. He also knew how fond Jane was of Emerald.

'Have you been introduced to Florence's guests of honour yet?' asked Hebden when there was a lull in the conversation. 'Aside from the Petries, that is.'

'No, we'd only just arrived when you saw us,' said de Silva. He grinned. 'In any case, although Jane may be, I'm not sure I'm sufficiently important.'

'Nonsense,' said Emerald. 'If David and I were introduced, I'm sure you and Jane will be. Not that it's a particularly enlivening experience,' she added in an undertone. 'Apparently, Walter and Grace Tankerton are immensely rich, but I'm afraid they're not lively company. He retired last year from some terribly important, and probably equally dull, job in banking. His wife is very reserved, and the daughter, Phoebe, hardly speaks.'

'What's brought them here?' asked Jane.

'Oh, they're travelling the world. They've been in India and wanted to visit Ceylon before they return to England.'

De Silva studied the family party, currently at the centre of a group being introduced to them by Florence. From a distance, none of the Tankertons appeared to be blessed with good looks. Grace Tankerton was a petite, bird-like woman with greying hair, who looked to be a good ten years younger than her husband. He too was thin and almost bald, with a walrus moustache; the pouches under his eyes spoke of long hours poring over paperwork. Both of them were conservatively dressed. Their daughter, Phoebe, wore an electric-blue frock that did nothing to flatter her complexion. She appeared to be taking no part in the conversation. Jane was a better judge of age than he was, but he guessed the girl wasn't more than eighteen or nineteen. A pity any youthful charm she might have had was spoiled by a sullen expression. Her age suggested to de Silva that the Tankertons had married late in life.

'Florence let her hair down to me the other day,' Emerald went on. 'She said that despite their huge fortune, the Tankertons don't seem very happy. Grace Tankerton is the more outgoing of the parents but even she's very quiet. As for the daughter, Phoebe, Florence isn't at all impressed with her. She says she has no conversation and behaves in a very wilful and obstinate way towards her parents. I think Florence may be rather relieved when the visit ends.'

De Silva wondered how the Tankertons felt about it. Florence was a good woman in many ways. For one thing, to use Jane's expression, she was no slacker. If there was a job to be done, she would do it, and do it well. Admittedly, she was inclined to be bossy, but she was generous if she realised someone needed help. He'd never have described her as a good listener though. In a group, unless she was overawed by the company, and he suspected that was rarely the case, she liked to hold the floor. Perhaps the Tankertons, rich as they were, found her rather overwhelming.

'Emerald, my dear,' remonstrated Hebden gently. 'I'm not sure you should say such things in public.'

Emerald giggled. 'You know I can't resist gossip. Anyway, Florence grants they do have a redeeming feature that, in her eyes, goes a long way towards excusing any amount of dullness.'

'What is it?' asked Jane.

'They've made an extremely generous donation to the orphanage.' Emerald whispered a figure behind her hand.

'Gracious. That is generous.'

If Florence was right about the Tankertons' fortune, reflected de Silva, they could probably well afford it. But one must give credit for generosity where it was due.

The conversation returned to the subject of interior decoration until the Hebdens left them to talk to other friends. 'Do you know,' said Jane when they were alone, 'all that talk of improvements makes me think it's time we made a few changes at Sunnybank.'

An alarming vision of paint pots and dustsheets rose before de Silva's eyes.

'Oh, there's no need to look so worried. Nothing as drastic as the Hebdens are doing. Just clearing out cupboards and drawers. I'm sure you don't need all those old gardening magazines you hoard.'

'I refer to them from time to time.'

'What? All of them?'

'Well, perhaps not... But what about all your film magazines?'

'Oh, I promise to prune them too.'

'Inspector de Silva! And Mrs de Silva! Good evening to you.'

The de Silvas turned to see William Petrie and his wife, Lady Caroline, beaming at them. Like Archie and all the other men from the British community, Petrie wore formal evening wear, but it sat much better on his tall, lean frame than Archie's did on his stouter one. Lady Caroline's evening gown was of a rich burgundy that complemented her ruby necklace. It was a very fine one. Aware that, unlike her husband, she came from one of the old, British aristocratic families, de Silva wondered if it was an heirloom.

'It's far too long since we've visited Nuala,' she remarked when they had exchanged greetings.

'Not so long for me, my dear,' remarked Petrie.

'Oh yes, I'm forgetting that dreadful business at the golf club.'

To de Silva, the golf club affair didn't seem all that long ago and was still quite fresh in his mind.

'The air is always so invigorating up here,' Lady Caroline went on. 'And it's delightful to see old friends. Tell me, Inspector, how is your garden?'

'There are always problems, ma'am – slugs and snails that eat my young plants, squirrels that dig holes in the lawn, or eat the apples and pears before they have a chance to ripen – but on the whole, I have no serious cause for complaint.'

'It sounds as if your complaints are very like those of the gardeners at Government House,' Lady Caroline said with a smile. 'I regularly have to commiserate with our head gardener.' She gestured to her husband. 'William can't understand what the fuss is about. He can barely tell a dahlia from a daisy. He'd turn the whole garden into fields and plant crops if I'd let him.'

Her husband chuckled. 'I won't deny I'd prefer to farm the land rather than cover it with lawns and flowerbeds.'

'Surely you would allow some flowers, sir?' asked Jane. 'I think there are few sights more lovely than poppies and cornflowers blowing in the wind in a field of corn.'

'You're quite right, Mrs de Silva. I'll allow poppies and cornflowers on this imaginary farm of mine. It's a dream I hope to turn into reality when we retire home to England one day. But that may not be for many years.'

'I'm glad to hear it,' said Jane. 'I'm sure that when the time comes, you'll be much missed.'

'It's good of you to say so, but I'm all too aware that no one is irreplaceable. Now, if you'll excuse us, we must go and speak to some of the other guests.'

'What a charming couple the Petries are,' said Jane, as they walked away. 'They never put on any airs and graces, although they're more entitled to do so than many people we know.'

De Silva laughed. 'Do you have someone in mind? Florence perhaps?'

Jane smiled. 'Now I know her better, it's easier to forgive Florence her faults.'

'I suppose I might say the same about Archie.' De Silva liked to think that their association over the years had slowly fostered a mutual respect.

'Heaven knows,' Jane went on, 'I'm sure I have many of my own.'

He squeezed her arm. 'Only your designs on my poor gardening magazines.'

A commotion at the entrance to the ballroom interrupted their conversation. A tall, strikingly handsome man, who de Silva guessed to be in his mid-forties, had arrived. The lady on his arm was clearly a good deal younger.

'They must be the O'Hallorans,' said Jane. 'I can tell you something about them because at the sewing circle last week, they provided the entire subject of Florence's conversation. They've been staying at the Crown Hotel, but now they're at the Residence for a few days. Miss O'Halloran is very beautiful, don't you think? And so elegantly dressed. She looks as if she's stepped out of a fashion magazine or one of those glorious portraits by John Singer Sargent, and her father is very handsome.'

Ah, father and daughter. De Silva gave himself a mental slap on the wrist for his uncharitable assumption. He studied the O'Hallorans more closely. The father's hair was impeccably groomed, but so black it was tempting to suspect it might be tinted. His daughter, also dark-haired, was tall with a willowy figure. Jane was right: the white ballgown she wore was spectacular, and she made a very charming sight.

'Hank O'Halloran is a millionaire,' Jane went on. 'Although Florence says that he claims he's not nearly as rich as Walter Tankerton. Apparently, his family came from

Ireland originally, but he was born in America. He makes no secret of the fact that his parents had very little money. Florence says he told her he had to pull himself up by his bootstraps.'

'It sounds painful.'

Jane smiled. 'Metaphorically speaking, dear. Anyway, I expect he and his daughter will liven up the party.'

'Is there a Mrs O'Halloran?'

'No. Sadly, she died many years ago.'

The O'Hallorans joined the group around the Tankertons and were swiftly greeted by a beaming Florence. The finer points of British etiquette frequently eluded de Silva, despite Jane's efforts to enlighten him, but presumably, if you were staying in the house, it wasn't a faux pas to join the party late and miss the receiving line. It had certainly provided them with the opportunity to make a grand entrance.

The atmosphere around the Tankertons, that had looked rather staid before the O'Hallorans' arrival, rapidly changed. Even the sullen Phoebe appeared to be enjoying herself. It wasn't long before Hank O'Halloran whisked her and his daughter away from the group and started to tour the room, introducing the three of them in such an easy manner that they might have been friends with most of the guests for years rather than new visitors to Nuala.

When they came to where Jane and de Silva stood, he wondered what they would find to talk about, but he needn't have worried. Both the O'Hallorans were so engaging, he soon forgot that he and Jane had only just met them. As Florence had observed, Phoebe Tankerton had little to say for herself, but she hung on the O'Hallorans' every word and laughed a great deal at Hank's jokes.

'Pa wanted me to have an expensive education,' Marie O'Halloran remarked when she heard that Jane had been a governess. 'But he might as well have saved his money. The school had as much chance of teaching me algebra and geometry as it did of getting a Minnesota moose to dance the tango.'

Hank O'Halloran tucked her arm in his and patted it fondly. 'I had to try.'

'I'm glad it didn't take too long to persuade you I was a lost cause. Life was much more fun after that. And what's the use of anything if you don't have fun?'

Her father chuckled. 'I'd never call you a lost cause, honey. You're smarter than most people I know.'

'We had fun yesterday, didn't we, Phoebe?' Marie O'Halloran went on. Phoebe nodded, but a cloud came over Hank O'Halloran's brow. 'Now, that wasn't such a smart thing to do. I don't like you girls going off gallivanting on the wrong side of town.'

Marie's chin jutted and de Silva glimpsed a strong will under the charm. 'We weren't on our own. We had Pat and Mrs Tankerton with us.' Her expression softened into a winning smile. 'And we came back, didn't we?'

'Where did you go?' asked Jane.

'To have our fortunes told. At least Phoebe and I did. The others wouldn't join in. I'd heard about a clairvoyant who'd do that for you.' Putting her arm through Phoebe's, Marie gave it a squeeze and laughed. 'It was such a lark, wasn't it, Phoebe darling?' She gave the assembled company a look of mock defiance. 'And it's no use asking what she said, because that's our little secret.'

De Silva wasn't sure he liked her attitude. The casting of horoscopes was held in high regard by many of the people of Ceylon. He recalled that, when he was growing up, the local astrologer had often come to the house at his mother's request when there was an important decision to be made. To de Silva's surprise, O'Halloran seemed to have the same reaction, for his severe expression didn't lighten.

'Don't make fun of people who see into the future, honey. Your great grandma used to read the stars. When your grandpa was born, she told everyone that one day he'd go to America and marry a woman with raven hair. They'd have a son who became a big success in business.' He paused then grinned. 'Well, here I am, and your grandma had black hair.'

He laughed and the atmosphere relaxed again. 'So, Inspector.' He turned to de Silva. 'I hear you're the guy who keeps us all safe in this little old town.'

De Silva's lips twitched. O'Halloran's friendliness was infectious. It was hard to take offence at Nuala being described in such a fashion. Anyway, on reflection, it was a small, and usually quiet place, and probably old by the standards of what he had heard about America.

'I do my best, sir.'

O'Halloran clapped him on the back. 'I'm sure we couldn't be in better hands. Now, if you'll excuse us, I think it's time Marie and I took Phoebe back to her folks. I see our lovely hostess getting ready to call us in for dinner, and I'm hungry enough to eat a bear.'

De Silva wasn't sure how palatable a bear would be, but he appreciated a man who acknowledged the demands of his stomach.

'An interesting man, Mr O'Halloran,' he observed to Jane as he led her into dinner after the gong had been struck. 'Unlike you British, it seems that Americans don't suffer from false modesty.'

'No, they don't, but from what I've heard, Hank O'Halloran's thoroughly entitled to be proud of his achievements.'

'By the way, who is this Pat?'

'Pat?'

'The person that Marie O'Halloran mentioned came with her and Phoebe to the clairvoyant.'

'I'm not sure.' She thought for a moment. 'Actually, he's probably the private secretary the Tankertons brought with them. Florence mentioned him. He's not really a secretary though, and his name's not really Pat, it's Patterson. Andrew Patterson. Florence said he's an ex-military man the Tankertons like to have around them to guard Phoebe, because they're terrified of kidnappers. If they're as rich as Florence says, that must be a real danger.'

'It must.'

De Silva remembered the tragic case of the kidnapping of the baby son of the famous aviator, Charles Lindbergh, a few years previously. It would have left many wealthy families alarmed.

'Still, they should be safe enough in Nuala,' Jane continued.

'I certainly hope so.'

* * *

At dinner, the Tankertons and the O'Hallorans were seated along the top of the U-shaped table with Archie, Florence, and the Petries, and, down each arm, several other couples de Silva recognised as belonging to the highest echelons of Nuala's small society. Along with the Hebdens and the remaining guests, Jane and de Silva had been placed on smaller, round tables within the U-shape. De Silva was interested to see that Phoebe Tankerton looked positively animated now. She and Marie O'Halloran were seated on either side of William Petrie, who also appeared to be enjoying himself.

Further along the table, Grace Tankerton listened politely to her neighbours, but de Silva noticed that her expression was careworn, and she cast frequent glances in her daughter's direction. It must be one thing accepting that you prepared your children to go out into the world and leave you behind – what was the British expression;

you cut the apron strings? – but another having to cope with the knowledge that your company gave them no pleasure whereas that of others did. Of course, it was possible that Grace Tankerton's sorrowful expression was due to the worry of needing someone to guard her daughter all the time. He thought of the man, Patterson, and wondered where he'd got to. Presumably, he was waiting discreetly somewhere, perhaps at another of the smaller tables, ready to spring into action if the need arose.

He turned his attention to his dinner. He never had high hopes of the meals served at the Residence, but tonight, with many Ceylonese guests, Florence had given the chef permission to tailor the menu to suit a wider variety of tastes than usual. The starter of devilled eggs was tasty, and a welcome choice between curried lamb, and roast leg with mint sauce, meant that de Silva left the table replete.

Returning to the ballroom, they found that the band had already started to play a medley of dance tunes. De Silva danced with Jane and then Emerald Hebden. 'I'm honoured that your husband allows me a few minutes of your company,' he said with a smile.

'Oh, David doesn't like dancing. He says he has two left feet. It's such a pity, because I love it.'

De Silva laughed. 'I'm sure the two left feet could be corrected if someone was sufficiently determined.'

'It will be my next project. Just as soon as the dining room's decorated.'

They passed close to the place where some of the older gentlemen sat out, enjoying their whisky and cigars. Archie was among them, talking to Walter Tankerton. It was nice to see Tankerton looking more at ease than he'd done earlier in the evening. De Silva wondered where the rest of his family were, then noticed Phoebe dancing with one of the Residence's young attachés. White columns with gilt capitals were spaced at intervals on either side of the ballroom, dividing it into three sections with the central one being the largest by far. He couldn't help himself thinking what any competent policeman would. Maybe this fellow Patterson was tucked behind one of them, his eyes never leaving his charge as she whirled through the throng in her partner's arms.

When the band took their break, de Silva was surprised to see Hank O'Halloran step up to the piano and start to play. Soon, an admiring circle formed around him as he took requests for people's favourite tunes, interspersing them with music the like of which de Silva had never heard before. Some people started to dance again.

'Ragtime,' said Jane appearing beside him, slightly out of breath from a turn around the floor with one of the young teachers at the government school. 'That was *The Maple Street Rag* by Scott Joplin.'

'It certainly sets the toes tapping.'

Jane fanned herself. 'I think I'm out of practice for dancing at that speed.'

'I don't know about that. I was most impressed.' He smiled. 'Albeit I prefer my wife to be dancing with me.'

They surveyed the dancers for a few moments then Jane glanced in the direction of the dais, where O'Halloran was still playing the piano. 'He plays very well, doesn't he? I don't really know why, but I didn't expect him to be musical.'

O'Halloran ended the piece with a flourish, and a burst of laughter rose from the audience around him at something he said. De Silva noticed that one of the ladies was Grace Tankerton who appeared to be enjoying herself at last. Another surprise.

'Shall we go a bit closer?' asked Jane. 'I'd love to watch him play.'

By the time they reached the group, O'Halloran had picked up a piece of music that lay on top of the piano.

'There's a great little duet in here. Would someone do me the honour of joining me?'

He swivelled to look at Grace Tankerton. 'How about you, ma'am? I know you play.'

Grace Tankerton flushed. 'Oh, I couldn't possibly.'

'Why not? We're among friends.'

She took a deep breath. 'Let me see the music.'

After she'd scanned it, she nodded. 'I suppose I'll manage, but please don't expect me to play fast.'

'I'm willing to bet you'd outplay me any day,' said O'Halloran with a grin. 'I started out playing in bars when I was first in Chicago. Honky-tonk tunes I expect people only half listened to. Still it paid the rent while I got on my feet. But you—' He smiled. 'Walter tells me that back home you play Beethoven, Mozart, Tchaikovsky – all the big guys.'

Grace Tankerton sat down beside him and flexed her fingers. When she began to play, she blossomed into a different creature: animated and carefree. After the last notes had died away, O'Halloran turned to her. 'Thank you,' he said softly.

It was at that moment that a jarring sound cut through the buzz of conversation and laughter. Groups of people nearest to the door to the reception hall stopped talking and looked to see where it had come from. The sound came again. This time, de Silva was sure it was a scream, and it came from the direction of the hall. Several other men followed him as he rushed out there.

Phoebe Tankerton stood at the top of the sweeping, double staircase, one hand clutching her throat. As de Silva reached her, she swayed and would have fallen if he hadn't caught her.

'Marie,' she said in an anguished whisper. 'They've taken Marie.'

CHAPTER 2

'We'd gone upstairs to Marie's room,' said Phoebe. De Silva had helped her the rest of the way downstairs, and now, they sat with her parents and Archie, who had just joined them, in the drawing room.

'Pat said it was alright as Marie was my friend. She wanted to powder her nose and I said I'd come too. She went to the bathroom first, then me, so she was on her own in the bedroom. When I saw her last, she was going to the French windows that lead out to the balcony to open them. She said she needed to cool off.'

A flood of sobs swallowed Phoebe Tankerton's voice. She took her mother's proffered handkerchief, blew her nose resolutely then dabbed her reddened eyes.

'You need to rest, dearest,' said Grace.

Her husband turned to de Silva. 'That's enough for the moment, Inspector,' he said, but Phoebe shook her head violently. 'Don't fuss, Father. I want to tell it all.'

'Well done, young lady,' said Archie approvingly. 'That's the spirit. What happened next?'

'I was in the bathroom when I heard Marie call my name and the sounds of a scuffle. I rushed to the bathroom door. At first, I thought that I'd been locked in, but then I realised that I was so frightened, I was trying to turn the handle the wrong way. I was calling out for Marie, but she didn't answer. As I pulled the bathroom door open the lights in the bedroom went out. I stepped forward and…'

She paused, a pulse in her cheek twitching, and her hands clenched in her lap.

'Can you tell us what happened then, Miss Tankerton?' asked de Silva gently.

'After the bright light in the bathroom, it seemed very dark. I sensed someone close by me. I didn't actually see them, but they grabbed me and put something over my face.' She shuddered. 'It smelled sickly. I remember that. I passed out, and when I came to, I was lying on the floor. I called Marie's name again, but she still didn't answer. I managed to get up and go to the light switch by the door to turn on the lights. The French windows were open—'

Another bout of sobbing overcame her. When it was over, her words came out in a croaky whisper. 'Marie was gone.'

Grace Tankerton stood up. 'Enough now. My daughter needs to rest. Let's go up to your room, Phoebe dear. I'll come and sit with you. I don't want anyone disturbing us,' she added firmly. 'You'll see to that, won't you, Walter?' She looked at her husband.

'I suggest you stay here, sir,' de Silva said to him as the ladies departed. He suspected that Walter Tankerton would be more of a hindrance in a search than an asset; close to, de Silva noticed a pallor in his face that suggested he wasn't in the best of health. 'I'm sure your wife and daughter will be reassured by your presence.'

A shrewd look came into Tankerton's eyes. He might be unfit, but he was no fool. De Silva hoped he hadn't taken offence. But then the banker nodded. 'Thank you, Inspector. I'm afraid I'm too old for running around in the dark. Patterson here,' he gestured towards a thickset, sandy-haired man who gave de Silva a chilly stare, 'will be much more help to you.' He nodded to Patterson. 'Phoebe's safe for the moment. Go and give a hand.' He shook his head sadly. 'Poor O'Halloran. I hope he finds his daughter unharmed. It's a bad business.'

'Indeed it is, sir.'

'I doubt the kidnappers will come here again tonight,' said Archie. 'But I've seen to it that some of our security men will be put on watch at the end of the corridor leading to your bedrooms and outside in the garden.'

'Thank you.'

Archie and de Silva left him and went out to the reception hall. Through the door to the ballroom, they saw that Jane and Lady Caroline were helping Florence Clutterbuck talk to the party guests to find out if they'd noticed anything untoward, before seeing them on their way.

'I suggested to my wife that they tick off departing guests on the guest list,' said de Silva quietly. 'Discreetly, of course.'

'Good thinking.' Archie sucked air between his teeth. 'Unpleasant to think the perpetrators may have been in our midst, but one can't be too careful. O'Halloran's already gone out with William Petrie and Frobisher.'

De Silva was glad to hear that Charlie Frobisher, one of Archie's younger staff, whose capabilities he greatly admired, was included in the search party.

'The Tankertons' man, Patterson, can join them,' Archie continued. 'I've also sent some of the servants with them to search the grounds, though what use they'll be with the kidnappers outwitting our security measures, I don't know. Now's not the time, but once the Tankertons have gone I'll be shaking things up in that department. Very embarrassing for me, of course. Meantime, I'd better go and do what I can to help. Are you coming, de Silva?'

'I'll follow you, sir. First, I'd like to contact Inspector Singh at Hatton. I have his home telephone number. Unfortunately, that's not the case for officers at the other police stations on the way to Kandy, and if the kidnappers have a car, they could be miles away by morning. All the same, it would be advisable to set up as many roadblocks as we can as soon as possible.'

'Good point. Before I go, I'll have one of the servants find a telephone for you to use. What about the train station?'

'I'll see to that in the morning. Nothing will be going down to Kandy until then. In any case, I doubt the kidnappers would take the risk of trying to spirit Miss O'Halloran away in a public place. Once I've got hold of Singh, I'd like to take another look at the bedroom Miss O'Halloran was abducted from and the area under the balcony.'

Archie nodded. 'Right. Let me know if you find anything illuminating.'

After he'd made the telephone call, de Silva went upstairs and combed the room Marie had been snatched from. He also checked the adjoining room used by Marie's father. Back in Marie's room, he sniffed a cushion that lay on the floor, close to where Phoebe remembered falling. The fabric gave off a sickly smell. He turned at the sound of the door opening to see Doctor Hebden.

'I've just been to visit Phoebe Tankerton and her mother. She wanted me to give the girl something to help her sleep. Thought I'd look in on my way back downstairs to see if I can be of any help.'

'That's very good of you.' De Silva held out the cushion. 'Do you detect anything?'

Hebden took a sniff. 'There's a distinct aroma. It might be chloroform, but a mixture of bleach and vinegar would have a similar smell and be far easier to obtain. Either would have been extremely unpleasant for the young lady. But of course, as I'm sure you're aware, it's a popular misconception among crime writers that holding something doused with chloroform over the victim's face is a simple and almost instantaneous method of rendering them unconscious. It is neither. I think it's far more likely that the young lady fainted because she was unable to breathe, and in a situation that terrified her.'

He looked about him. 'I've never been upstairs in the Residence before. If this is a good example, the bedrooms are very fine.' He pointed to a door. 'Where does that lead to?'

'The bedroom occupied by Marie O'Halloran's father. There's a balcony that also unites the rooms, with access through French windows from both of them.' He dusted off his hands. 'I think I've about finished here. Apart from the cushion, there's nothing that might give us any clues, either in the rooms or on the balcony.'

'A nice tidy job, eh,' said Hebden grimly. 'From what I've seen of her, Marie O'Halloran's no shrinking violet. I think she'd have put up a fight if she could, so maybe she was drugged too.'

'Very probably.'

De Silva went to the door. 'I need to fetch a torch from my car, then I'm going to have a look at the area below the balcony. If nothing else, there may be footprints that show us how many people we're dealing with.'

'I may as well go and see if I can help with the search of the grounds. The Applebys have taken Emerald home.'

'I'll join you when I've finished.'

* * *

Armed with the torch he always carried in the Morris's glove compartment, de Silva walked around to the south side of the Residence, soon finding the place he wanted.

The gardeners must have watered earlier that day. It hadn't rained for weeks, but the soil in the flowerbed under the balcony was damp. It was also churned up and flowers had been trampled leaving their broken-off heads lying limp on the ground.

A well-established magnolia covered the wall. Examining it by the light of his torch, de Silva saw it had thick branches. He reached for one of them and gave it a shake. The leathery leaves rustled but the sturdy framework held firm. It would not have been hard for an agile person to climb up to the balcony and back down again, even carrying or lowering down a drugged victim.

He shone the torch on the disturbed soil. He was sure there were two sets of footprints: one pair larger than the other but both too large to belong to Marie. Two kidnappers then. Yes, one must have lowered Marie down from the balcony and then they carried her as they made their escape. She was slim, so she wouldn't have been an impossible burden.

Making one last sweep with the torch beam, he wondered how the kidnappers had known which room to aim for. That was something he would need to find out. Sadly, he was not surprised that the kidnappers had evaded the Residence's security. In his experience, the quality of personnel involved in such duties was not high. At first sight, it indicated inside knowledge of the Residence, but he'd need more than assumptions if he was to accuse anyone. Also, why not kidnap both girls, and, if practicalities dictated that it had to be just one, why Marie rather than Phoebe? After all, if what he'd heard was true, Tankerton could afford a larger ransom than O'Halloran. Clearly there was more to this crime than simple opportunism.

He was on his way back to the front of the Residence when he met Archie.

'Anything to report, de Silva?' The assistant government agent looked weary. Darcy, the Labrador, at his master's heels as usual, wagged his tail, but he too looked as if he longed for his bed.

'Only that I'm fairly certain the kidnappers made their escape over the balcony, sir, and there were two of them.'

'Hmm. Not much help, I fear. We've had no luck yet either. I brought O'Halloran back with me. He's bearing up admirably, but we don't want this going on much longer. These first few hours are likely to be the most vital for finding Marie O'Halloran. I think we can be sure the kidnappers aren't in the grounds now. There are plenty of places where the perimeter wall could be climbed. William Petrie and young Frobisher have taken that chap, Patterson, and some of the servants to have a look around on the other side of it. See if they can find where the kidnappers got over. Have you managed to do anything about those roadblocks?'

'I spoke to Inspector Singh, and he offered to take responsibility for that. At this hour, he may not be able to get hold of everyone needed, but he's promised to do his best. I don't think we can ask for more.'

Archie sighed. 'I agree. Have you seen anything of the Tankertons? Do you know how they're bearing up?'

'The ladies haven't come downstairs. Doctor Hebden told me that Mrs Tankerton asked him to give Phoebe something to make her sleep. I'm not sure where her father has got to.'

'Poor old Tankerton, I don't think he's up to this kind of thing. Mind you, I'm not sure I am. I'm not getting any younger. Just as well Frobisher's here. Another couple of weeks and he would have been on annual leave, climbing some peak or other in the Himalayas. Tankerton's man, Patterson, seems a useful sort of chap too. Tankerton mentioned to me before all this business blew up that Patterson served with distinction during the war. After demob, he needed work, and a former officer in his regiment recommended him, so Tankerton took him on for security duties. It's a black mark against him though that he wasn't on hand when Marie was snatched.'

He stifled a yawn. 'Right then. We'd better be getting on with things. O'Halloran's waiting for us in my study.'

CHAPTER 3

Passing the ballroom once more, de Silva glimpsed Florence, Jane, and Lady Caroline still busy with the last of the party guests. The room had a forlorn look now. The Residence's servants who hadn't gone on the search had cleared up glasses and straightened chairs, but the dance band's music stands remained on the dais, scattered around the piano like an audience of weary skeletons.

Hank O'Halloran sat in Archie's study. The flamboyant, lively air had vanished, and he looked exhausted and haggard.

'You mustn't give up hope, man,' said Archie briskly. 'We'll find her.'

O'Halloran shot him a sceptical look. 'Good of you to say so, Clutterbuck, but you know as well as I do how these things often end.'

He slapped the arm of the chair with the palm of his hand, leaving a damp patch on the polished mahogany. 'It's my fault. All my fault.'

De Silva recognised the reaction. In his experience, the families of a victim, particularly the fathers, frequently blamed themselves for not keeping their loved one safe.

'Now, now; I'm sure there's no justification for that.' Clutterbuck spoke in a soothing voice de Silva hadn't often heard.

O'Halloran's eyes blazed. 'Oh, but there is. What the

hell do you—' He stopped and dragged a hand over his face. 'I apologise. You can't have known.'

He fell silent, as if he had forgotten they were there. Exchanging glances, de Silva and Archie waited for him to resume.

'I've been getting letters,' he said at last. 'Threatening letters.' He let out a bitter exclamation. 'God help me, I laughed them off and told my secretary to tear them up. No man who makes a success in business escapes without making enemies.'

De Silva wasn't sure that was always true, but perhaps it applied in O'Halloran's line of work. At least that might explain why Marie was the target, not Phoebe. The motive could be personal.

'May I ask what these letters said, sir?'

'Variants on a theme – I have a beautiful daughter; it would be a tragedy if anything happened to her. That kind of veiled threat.'

'Was there anything about the letters that provided a clue as to who wrote them?'

O'Halloran shook his head. 'They were never handwritten. The author used a typewriter, and the paper was cheap quality. Could have been bought anywhere.'

'As you've been travelling, sir, how did you receive the letters?'

'They were delivered to hotels we stayed at after we got to India. I can only assume the writer had somehow familiarised himself with our itinerary. Maybe he was following us from place to place.'

'Did you report the letters to the police at any of the places you stayed?'

O'Halloran shrugged. 'I thought about it but decided there would be no point. What would they have done? The cities we stayed in were big – Delhi, Bombay, Calcutta to name a few – and the letters were delivered with the general post, not by messenger. Even if they had been, I doubt the hotel receptionists would have asked the messengers for the name of the sender. In any case, as I said, I didn't take them seriously.'

'And did you tell anyone else about the letters?'

'No one – apart from my secretary, as I said,' O'Halloran replied bitterly. 'My secretary knows when to keep silent, and I didn't want to frighten Marie unnecessarily.'

'Understandable,' intervened Archie. 'Shall we move on?'

Part of de Silva was relieved that he wasn't faced with the need to contact police forces all over India.

'Do you have any idea how the kidnappers would have known you were staying at the Residence, sir?' he asked.

'I suppose that's a question for me too,' said Archie. 'The office staff and the servants knew, of course, but nearly all of them have been with us for years, and I'd vouch for their honesty, if not their efficiency. I'll see to it, however, that you have the opportunity to question anyone you want. Mr O'Halloran and his daughter have been staying here to facilitate the early starts to the hunting and fishing expeditions he's been taking part in. Again, the other participants are well known to me. I'd be surprised if they have anything to conceal.'

'But possibly they talked about who was in the party and word reached the wrong ears,' said de Silva.

'Possible, I suppose. But it'll be a tall order for them to remember their every conversation in the run up to the trips.' He turned to O'Halloran. 'Might you or your daughter have mentioned to anyone that you were staying here?'

'I don't recall doing so, but Marie may have.'

In the silence that fell, de Silva reflected that there were so many potential avenues of inquiry as to be of doubtful use.

'If you're going to ask me how whoever did this knew which room to pick,' O'Halloran went on, 'Marie and I

27

didn't exactly keep our whereabouts a secret. Didn't think we needed to.' He glanced at Archie. 'No offence intended.'

Archie cleared his throat uncomfortably. 'None taken.'

'We breakfasted on the balcony each morning and stood out there to get a breath of fresh air in the evenings before and after going down to dinner. Anyone watching from the grounds had plenty of opportunity to work out where we were.'

And this evening, de Silva reflected, with crowds of people around and a relaxed party atmosphere, it had been the perfect opportunity to snatch Marie. The kidnappers only needed to conceal themselves on the balcony and wait for her to come up to her room. If she'd not left the party when she did but come to bed at the same time as her father, their task would have involved more risk. They would have needed to remain hidden until O'Halloran was safely in his own room, but de Silva recalled a clutch of potted palms on the balcony that would have served. However, luck had been on their side. It was not O'Halloran who was with Marie, but Phoebe. Although the kidnappers may not have known she was in the bathroom when they first grabbed Marie, Phoebe had proved an easy obstacle to deal with. Most likely they had no idea who she was. Marie was the one with the star quality appearance.

'Inspector de Silva has arranged for roadblocks to be set up between here and Kandy,' Archie said, dragging de Silva's thoughts back to the present. 'He'll mount a full police search in the morning.' He turned to de Silva. 'You'd better call up reinforcements from Kandy and any of the towns in between that can spare policemen.'

Noticing that O'Halloran didn't look too keen, de Silva wondered why.

'Have no fear,' Archie ended. 'We'll find her.'

O'Halloran shook his head. 'Back off is the advice I've always heard. The consequences can be disastrous if these people get jumpy. You have to play the game according to their rules. There'll be a ransom demand before long, and I intend to pay it.'

De Silva heard Archie's sharp intake of breath.

O'Halloran shook his head. 'Hear me out. It's taking too much of a risk with Marie's life to try and track down the kidnappers at this stage. I want my daughter back with me, then I'll hand over to you, and you can do what the hell you please.'

There was a knock at the door. Archie called out and a servant entered. 'Memsahib Tankerton would like to speak with you, sahib.'

'Show her in.'

Archie got to his feet as she entered. 'Mrs Tankerton, I wasn't expecting to have the pleasure of seeing you again tonight. Is your husband not with you? I hope he's bearing up.'

Grace Tankerton raised an eyebrow. 'I must say, the word pleasure doesn't seem an appropriate one for this evening but thank you. And thank you for asking after Walter. I'm afraid all this has exhausted him, so I've persuaded him to rest.'

Momentarily, Archie looked chastened and de Silva felt a little sorry for him. 'How is Phoebe?' he asked, recovering.

'Still asleep. Your doctor gave her something to help with that, but I fear she's bound to be very distressed when she wakes.' She turned to Hank O'Halloran. 'She's extremely fond of your dear daughter; all three of us are.'

Hank O'Halloran and de Silva had also risen to their feet at her entrance. O'Halloran went over to her and took her hand. 'That means more to me than I can say. I—' His shoulders slumped; he remained beside her, holding tightly to her hand as if it was the only thing standing between him and total despair.

Gently, Grace Tankerton touched his cheek. 'You must be brave, you know. Marie needs you to be brave.'

His head jerked up. 'How?' he asked fiercely. 'How can I be brave? Marie's all I have. If I lose her, I'll go crazy.' A sob shook his frame, and Grace folded him in her arms. Glancing at Archie, de Silva saw that his boss was torn between pity and embarrassment. Clearly, the Americans didn't share the British habit of the stiff upper lip, or at least this American didn't.

Grace Tankerton was talking in a soothing voice, responding to something O'Halloran was saying, but the words were inaudible. Eventually, O'Halloran allowed her to lead him to a sofa and they sat down, side by side.

'Well, Mr Clutterbuck?' she asked. 'Inspector? Do you really think it's advisable to start a search at this point? I agree with Mr O'Halloran. Much the best and safest way is to wait until we have Marie back with us, then you may pursue these criminals.'

Archie shifted his weight uneasily. 'I understand your point of view, ma'am, but we have to consider the fact that there have been cases where a victim's family have paid the ransom in vain.'

O'Halloran shot Archie an angry look. 'Are you trying to tell me you think she's dead already?'

'My dear chap, nothing of the kind, I assure you. I merely meant that we ought to use all the resources at our disposal if we're to rescue your daughter.'

'And I disagree. I won't take the risk. Whatever they ask, I'll pay it.' He glared at Archie. 'I want your word on this, sir. You don't move a muscle until my daughter's back with me. You too, Inspector. No heroics, understood?'

De Silva studied the American's expression. This man meant what he said, and he might well have a point. If these kidnappers were ruthless, it was not beyond the bounds of possibility that if they thought there was an attempt to trick them, they would take their revenge. He looked sideways at Archie. His boss's face showed a mixture of indecision

30

and displeasure. He wasn't used to being gainsaid. De Silva suspected that he was all at sea over how to deal with this novel experience.

Archie swallowed hard. 'Very well. If that's your decision, I hope I speak for everyone when I say we won't stand in your way. Provided,' he gave O'Halloran a hard stare, 'that afterwards, you let us deal with it in ours. We mustn't forget that the safety of others may be at risk.'

CHAPTER 4

It was nearly dawn when de Silva and Jane emerged from the Residence and went to fetch the Morris and drive home, leaving the others to try to get some rest.

'Lady Caroline, Florence, and I managed to account for all the guests,' said Jane.

'That's something. At least we can be sure that none of them ran off with our victim.' He knuckled the tiredness out of his eye. 'Although I suppose we shouldn't discount the possibility of there being an accomplice among them. It may not be the case that the kidnappers had to wait on the balcony for however long it took for Marie to come back to her room.'

'You mean there was some sort of prearranged signal?'

'It's possible.' He sighed.

'It sounds as if you haven't made as much progress as you would like.'

'Regrettably not, and these early hours after a kidnap are often the most important. Petrie, Charlie Frobisher, Patterson, and the rest of the search party had no luck. I only hope Inspector Singh has managed to set up the roadblocks, although if the kidnappers planned to make their escape through the jungle, watching the roads may do us no good.'

'Surely, they'll have to pass through some kind of a settlement eventually, even if it's only a small one.'

'But would the inhabitants report them to the authorities? And even if they decided to do so, these places in the back of beyond rarely have any speedy means of communication.'

'That's true.'

'In any case, the kidnappers may be relying on O'Halloran paying the ransom. They may not have gone far but are well hidden.'

'I hope they don't mistreat her,' said Jane anxiously. 'She seems an independent young woman, but I doubt anything in her life has prepared her for coping with an eventuality such as this.'

'I doubt anything in most people's lives would,' said de Silva dryly.

'The Tankertons must be very relieved their daughter is safe. I wonder why the kidnappers didn't take her too. I suppose they weren't expecting her to be there and may not know that her family's wealthy anyway. After all, from what I hear, the Tankertons don't generally go out of their way to advertise their wealth. Not that I mean Hank O'Halloran does so in a vulgar way,' she added hastily. 'But he is a more flamboyant character.'

'Sadly, his high spirits are decidedly dimmed at the moment,' said de Silva. 'But in any case, I think there's a different reason why the kidnappers left Phoebe.' He explained about the letters.

'So, it may be someone the O'Hallorans know. Perhaps someone who has a personal grudge,' said Jane when he had finished.

'Either or both seem possible. I'd like a word with O'Halloran's secretary at some point to see if she can come up with any suggestions. O'Halloran's angry with himself now for not taking the threats seriously, but otherwise, he was dismissive on the subject. He just said he didn't think the letters important at the time, and that anyone who's successful in business makes enemies.'

'I feel dreadfully sorry for poor Phoebe Tankerton. In a rare moment, her mother confided a few days ago to Florence that she was glad Phoebe and Miss O'Halloran had become good friends. The O'Hallorans and the Tankertons have travelled together for some time now, although they didn't set out from England together. Florence says Grace Tankerton seems to worry a lot about her daughter's happiness. I suppose it must be hard being the daughter of such a wealthy family, and the only child at that. It may not help that the Tankertons are quite elderly parents. I suspect Phoebe hasn't many friends of her own age. A life hedged about by the dangers great wealth imposes must be lonely at times.'

'I suppose it must, although on a policeman's salary, I doubt I'll ever know.'

Jane laughed. 'We do perfectly well. I wouldn't change a thing.'

He smiled and stifled a yawn. 'Thank you, my love.' He glanced towards the eastern horizon where a thin line of gold divided the earth and the sky. 'It's been a long night.'

'You aren't going to try to do anything else until you've had some sleep, are you?'

'No, it would be most inadvisable.'

The Morris turned into the drive at Sunnybank. The rising sun suffused the low-lying clouds with rose and gold. The soft, azure sky shimmered. Already conducting their dawn chorus, birds flitted from tree to tree. As he climbed out of the car and went around to help Jane, de Silva shivered. He wasn't sure whether it was just the early morning chill or the prospect of this business going horribly wrong.

CHAPTER 5

He snatched a few hours' sleep then dressed and drove down to the station. A call to the police at Hatton established that Inspector Singh had been successful in setting up the roadblocks in his area and contacting other stations, but there was no sign of the kidnappers so far. De Silva thanked him, and Singh promised to let him know if there was any news.

'And if I'm not here at the station,' said de Silva, 'you should be able to reach me at the Residence.'

'Well, good luck,' said Singh in his gravelly voice. 'This kind of case is notoriously difficult to deal with.'

When he had put the telephone down, de Silva stared glumly at the blotter on his desk for a few moments. Singh was right, but perhaps O'Halloran's method of dealing with the problem would ease the way. If he hadn't been so insistent, de Silva would have sent Prasanna and Nadar house to house by now, to make inquiries as to whether anyone had noticed a car driving through town late at night, or seen a woman answering to Marie O'Halloran's description, but he must resist until after the kidnappers made contact and Marie was found. If she was found.

Later was also the time for asking locally about any suspicious activities in the days running up to the kidnap. Had anybody noticed someone new to town? Nuala was a small enough place for a stranger to be remarked on, especially if they asked questions about the Residence.

One thing he did do, however, was alert the station master at Nanu Oya, who promised to telephone the police station immediately if there was any suspicious activity. If the kidnappers were still in town, de Silva didn't want them slipping away by train, unlikely as it seemed that they would try. At least he could discount escape by water. There was no navigable river for a hundred miles; the town lake was fed from an underground source.

As lunchtime approached, it occurred to him that there was one avenue he might explore without taking any risks. The deputy manager at the Crown Hotel was an old friend who had recently moved up to Nuala. It would be easy enough to slip in by the kitchen entrance to the hotel and join him for lunch. After a discreet telephone call to the hotel, he set off.

The Gunesekera family had lived in the bungalow next door to the de Silvas when de Silva was growing up in Colombo. He and their youngest son, Sanjeewa, had been boyhood friends and still kept up their friendship, even though their lives had gone in very different directions. Sanjeewa Gunesekera had married a local lady and together, they had produced a large brood of children. Out of affection for his old friend, de Silva endeavoured to remember their names and ages when the two of them met but soon gave up the unequal struggle. Fortunately, this never seemed to cause offence. Sometimes, de Silva wondered whether such a life would have suited him, but he always concluded that life without Jane was unthinkable.

Behind the scenes at the Crown, Sanjeewa welcomed him warmly. Lunchtime service was in full swing. Coming from the direction of the huge, steamy kitchen area, a cacophony of shouted orders and clattering pans made it hard for de Silva to hear what his friend was saying, but as he followed him down a corridor to a quieter place, conversation became easier.

'I've told them to bring us a selection of dishes,' said Sanjeewa. 'Not forgetting your favourite pea and cashew curry, of course.'

De Silva chuckled. 'Thank you.'

Sanjeewa's office was a good size; its furnishings included a table placed in front of the window with a chair either side. The view from there over the area where delivery trucks came and went was very different to the ones that the hotel guests enjoyed, but de Silva found it interesting to see the nuts and bolts of a large hotel. There were crates for fruit and vegetables piled high; metal kegs, that presumably held beer; stacks of wood; laundry carts; enormous bins for rubbish, and broken furniture awaiting disposal.

'I've made a few inquiries,' said Sanjeewa when they were sitting down. 'But only among staff I rely on as being absolutely trustworthy, I assure you.'

De Silva nodded. 'Thank you.'

'None of them have noticed—'

He broke off at a knock at the door. 'Come in!'

A waiter with a white napkin over one arm entered, pushing a small trolley laden with dishes. As he laid them out on the table, enticing smells of spices, coconut, and grilled fish rose to de Silva's nostrils.

'You may go,' said Sanjeewa when the waiter had found space for the final dish. 'We'll serve ourselves.'

The waiter left and Sanjeewa handed de Silva a serving spoon. 'Dig in. Now, as I was saying, none of them noticed anyone hanging around or asking questions about the O'Hallorans. Interestingly enough, despite what you told me about these threatening letters, there were no letters at all for them while they were at the Crown.'

Indeed, that was interesting. De Silva thought about it as he added pea and cashew curry, and then fish in a hot, red curry sauce, to the mound of steaming rice on his plate. The crispy-skinned pieces of fish were a deep, golden brown flecked with black, just as he liked them.

'Do you think the kidnappers wanted O'Halloran to lower his guard?' asked Sanjeewa.

'That might be the reason. If so, it was a clever move. O'Halloran told me he never took the letters seriously in the first place. He deeply regrets that now. If they stopped coming, it was probably quite easy for him to put them out of his mind, even after a few days of not getting any.'

They ate in silence for a few moments. 'This fish is very good,' said de Silva at last, pointing to one of the remaining morsels on his plate with his fork.

'I'll tell the chef. He will be pleased. He does his best with all the British food he has to prepare, but naturally, he is much happier cooking our own dishes. I'm glad to say that some of the British have developed a taste for them, although with less chilli than you or I would choose. More often though, they want roasted or grilled meat, and vegetables boiled to extinction. The food they grew up with.'

'To be fair, most of us prefer something familiar on our plates.'

Sanjeewa shrugged. 'That's one way of looking at it.'

From their different perspectives, both de Silva and his friend had plenty of opportunity in their work to study the British. However, due to the English newspapers that the hotel ordered in for its residents, Sanjeewa tended to be more aware of what was going on in the wider world outside Ceylon. As he talked of the situation in England and the growing concern in some quarters about the German chancellor, Herr Hitler, de Silva's mind was only half on what his friend was saying. He was more interested in why the letters had ceased coming. Was there something he was missing?

'The world is changing, my friend,' finished Sanjeewa then looked at de Silva quizzically. 'You've not heard a word I've been saying, have you?'

De Silva gave him an apologetic smile. 'Something about India winning her independence?'

'Ah, you did hear something. Then I said that when it happens, Ceylon is sure to follow.'

'You really think India will win her independence?'

'Yes, it's only a matter of time.' Sanjeewa smiled. 'I know you mistrust change, my friend, but no one can stand in the way of progress.'

'I only distrust change if it is too rapid. There is nothing to be gained and much to be lost by throwing the baby out with the bathwater.'

'Certainly not the baby,' said Sanjeewa with a chuckle.

De Silva pushed his plate away. 'Delicious, but I will stop there.'

'Neither of us have the appetites we had when we were young,' said Sanjeewa sadly.

'Nor the waistlines.'

'Very true.'

'Thank you again for your help. And for an excellent meal. I'll leave you to get on with your work. If any letters come addressed to Mr O'Halloran, I'd be grateful if you would notify me immediately.'

'Of course. Poor fellow – he must be in a great deal of distress.'

'He is. As I told you, he's determined to pay whatever the kidnappers demand in exchange for his daughter. I only hope nothing will go wrong.'

'Well, I assure you, nothing will get out about this meeting.'

'Thank you.'

* * *

Back at the station, de Silva telephoned the Residence. Archie Clutterbuck was in a meeting but Charlie Frobisher, who came on the line, told him that no ransom demand had been received.

'Nothing at the Crown either,' said de Silva, going on to explain what he'd learnt from Sanjeewa Gunesekera. 'How is Mr O'Halloran bearing up?'

'As well as can be expected. The Tankertons are very solicitous with him, particularly Mrs Tankerton. She's turned out to be surprisingly motherly where he's concerned. When Florence suggested the family stay on for a few days longer than planned, she accepted readily. I think she wants to keep an eye on him. I can't fathom the daughter, Phoebe, though. She's a strange girl. Sulky around her parents, although she brightened up when she was in the O'Hallorans' company. Clearly, she's very upset about Marie O'Halloran being kidnapped.'

De Silva thought of the wistful looks he had noticed Grace Tankerton give her daughter at Florence's party. If that famous British stiff upper lip extended to the relationship between mother and daughter, it must make it hard to understand each other. Then again, according to Jane, Florence had described Phoebe as obstinate and wilful. Whether deliberately or unconsciously, she might be making life hard for her mother. Thankfully, not being a parent, it was a problem with which he wasn't likely to need to concern himself.

'Walter Tankerton doesn't say a lot and keeps himself to himself most of the time,' Charlie Frobisher continued. 'I think he's not in very good health.'

'Yes, I thought the same at the party.'

'He likes to sit in the shade in the grounds, puffing on his pipe and looking through the newspapers. Checking the value of his stocks and shares, no doubt.'

'Do you think he's far richer than Mr O'Halloran?'

'Oh, I think so. We don't have all the lowdown on Tankerton, but I'm pretty certain he's very close to the top of the British list so far as business fortunes go.'

De Silva tried unsuccessfully to suppress a yawn.

'It was a long night, wasn't it,' said Frobisher sympathetically.

'Yes.' De Silva realised that the benefits of his morning nap had already worn off. 'I may go home for an hour or two. Will you telephone me if there's any news?'

'Of course.'

* * *

Before returning to Sunnybank, he spent a few minutes with Sergeant Prasanna and Constable Nadar. He realised that they knew nothing of what had been happening, so he filled them in.

'Is there anything you want us to do, sir?' asked Prasanna.

'At the moment, there's nothing. We have to play this one very carefully. But if anyone calls here, I want to hear about it straight away, so at least one of you had better stay at the desk all the time.' He gestured to a stack of files. 'There are plenty of things to be getting on with there.'

Both his sergeant and his constable looked disconsolate. He was sure they would like to be more involved and given something more exciting to do than deal with routine paperwork. He promised them that as soon as a suitable opportunity came up, they would be.

At Sunnybank, there was no sign of Jane. Then he remembered it was her afternoon for the sewing circle. Life in Nuala went on; indeed there must be many of its inhabitants who weren't even aware of the drama in their midst. And if they were, they might not find it a matter of great concern either. For a large proportion of them, their world revolved around making ends meet, the care of their families and, if they were lucky enough to have a patch of land, the success or failure of this year's harvest. Taking his mind back to the conversation with his friend, Sanjeewa, he couldn't help thinking that even the question of independence for Ceylon probably troubled their waking hours infrequently, if ever. What were those lines that Shakespeare wrote? He rummaged in his memory and found them:

There is a tide in the affairs of men,
Which taken at the flood, leads on to fortune,
Omitted, all the voyage of their life is bound in
shallows and miseries.

He hesitated to argue with the bard, but experience had shown that not all tides led to good fortune. Some swept away villages and livelihoods. Naturally, no sensible person desired misery, but many were perfectly happy to spend their days pottering about in the shallows of life, even if those shallows were, in the case of Ceylon, ruled by the British.

And talking of pottering, he decided that was just what he needed: an hour of fresh air out in the garden. Telling one of the servants to call him in immediately if anyone telephoned, he went out by the French windows.

A wander around the vegetable garden gave him the satisfaction of seeing that his newly planted leeks were already thrusting robust green shoots through the soil. In the rows nearby, earthy red beetroots shouldered their way through the soil, and green, scaly marrows lay entangled in their rambling foliage. Scarlet flowers brightened the runner beans festooning a row of bamboo poles. Closer inspection revealed tiny green commas that, in a few weeks, would swell to a harvestable size. Jane always said that gardening in England proceeded in slow motion compared to the time it took to grow a crop in Ceylon.

At the door to the potting shed, he stopped; it hung slightly ajar. Anif, their gardener, must have forgotten to latch it properly. He must have another word with him. Squirrels and small rodents could do considerable damage if they got in.

He peered around the door and groaned. That was exactly what had happened. The terracotta flowerpots that had been neatly stacked along the shelves on the back wall of the shed had been knocked over, and some lay in pieces on the floor. Packets of seeds were scattered about; partly unravelled, the ball of garden twine that he kept on a hook had been teased into a tangle that would, almost certainly, have resulted in a different outcome to the story of Theseus and Ariadne.

He opened the door wider and was wondering whether to tidy up the place himself, or tell Anif to deal with it, when he heard one of the servants. The man hurried over to him.

'There is a telephone call, sahib.'

'I'll come.'

It was Frobisher again.

'The ransom note has arrived,' he said. 'It came in the afternoon post, postmarked Nuala and posted this morning. It looks like the kidnappers haven't gone very far. Can you get up here?'

'I'm on my way.'

CHAPTER 6

He drove over to the Residence and joined William Petrie, Archie, and Hank O'Halloran in Archie's study.

'What did I tell you?' asked O'Halloran. 'They warn me not to involve the police. I hope it's not a mistake even getting you up here.'

Jabbing his finger at a place in the letter, he passed it to de Silva who, frowning, started to read.

Archie gave a snort of disgust. 'They have the nerve to say that this is the kind of thing that's best settled between gentlemen. Gentlemen, indeed!'

De Silva continued to read: *You must bring the money in a plain bag. Come to the wayside shrine five miles beyond Nuala on the Hatton road. Leave your car there and walk a hundred paces due west. Turn and walk a hundred paces due north. You will come to a clearing. Hand over the bag to the man who meets you there. Once the money has been counted, your daughter will be returned to you. Remember that if you try any tricks she will suffer for it.*

To de Silva, the manner of expression indicated that the writer spoke English as their first language. He folded the letter and handed it back to O'Halloran. 'They're asking for a great deal of money, sir. Can you raise it?'

'If it takes my last buck.'

'But by the day after tomorrow?' interjected Archie. 'It doesn't give you much time.'

'I'll manage.' O'Halloran grimaced. 'I'll have to, won't I? They say there's no point asking for more time. There isn't going to be a second chance.'

Seeing the misery in O'Halloran's eyes raised a lump in de Silva's throat. The American was right: he had no choice. The kidnappers held all the cards.

He knew the shrine and had often passed it on the way to Hatton. It consisted of a small wooden structure with a roof but no walls. A wooden statue of the Buddha – much cracked and weathered with age – stood on the platform inside. Passing travellers sometimes left offerings of flowers or food, but for the most part, it was neglected. It was a strange place to choose, since only one road led to it. Possibly the kidnappers planned to make their escape through the jungle. If so, their local knowledge must be good. They'd need to travel at least five miles before there was a likelihood of finding a decent track, let alone another road.

O'Halloran scraped back his chair, got up and paced to the far end of the study. He stood still for a few moments while the others waited for him to speak then swung round and slammed a clenched fist into the palm of his other hand.

'Don't any of you try to stop me. My mind is made up. I'll need a car to get down to the bank in Colombo. Can that be fixed?'

'Of course,' said Petrie. 'You'll arrange it, won't you, Clutterbuck?'

'At once, sir. And a driver, I assume.'

'No driver,' said O'Halloran sharply. 'I'm not taking any chances.'

Petrie frowned. 'With respect, you're not used to the roads over here. There'll be no one to help you if you get into trouble.'

'I've driven enough dirt roads back home to know what

I'm doing. I'm used to not seeing a gasoline station or a town for miles.'

'Will you at least agree to some of us waiting close to the shrine?' asked Petrie. 'Provided we stay out of view, of course. It would give us a better chance of pursuing the kidnappers once you have your daughter safely back.'

'I'll have to think about it.'

'If I may intervene, sir,' said de Silva gently. 'I appreciate that the letters you received contained threats against your family personally, but I think it would be unwise to discount the possibility that these people may one day present a danger to others as well.'

O'Halloran's brow furrowed. De Silva noticed how the veins in his neck bulged above the crisp, white shirt collar. 'Very well,' he growled. 'I agree they need to be caught. Once a crook, always a crook, eh? But just make sure you don't move a muscle until I tell you Marie's safe. If there are any mistakes, her blood will be on your hands.'

The ice in his voice sent a chill through the room; an uncomfortable silence fell. De Silva wondered whether Archie or William Petrie would remonstrate with O'Halloran. Perhaps the reason they didn't was the American's obvious distress. But if the plan went wrong, what lengths would he go to get his revenge? He hoped they didn't have to find out.

* * *

'That was an ugly moment,' said Archie. De Silva noticed that his hand was unsteady as he took a cigarette from the box on his desk and lit up.

'I don't blame O'Halloran for his attitude,' said William Petrie calmly. 'But provided we're careful, nothing will go wrong. One thing I'm sure of is that we can't let these people remain at large. There's the general good to consider.' He turned to de Silva. 'What's your view on the motive here? A personal vendetta, money, or both?'

'The letters lead me to believe it's personal, sir, but I agree with you; as I indicated to Mr O'Halloran, we can't ignore the issue of general safety. If the motive is financial and the kidnappers discover how wealthy the Tankertons are, Miss Tankerton would be at risk.'

Petrie nodded. 'Quite; if Marie O'Halloran was a prize for the kidnappers, think how much greater a one Phoebe Tankerton would be.'

Granted, she had Andrew Patterson to protect her, thought de Silva, but his performance so far hadn't been very reassuring. If it hadn't been for their concern for Hank O'Halloran, de Silva suspected the Tankertons would have left Nuala by now.

'You know the country around here best of any of us, de Silva,' William Petrie went on. 'If the kidnappers intend to leave the hills, as I imagine they do, what direction do you think they'll take after they've handed Marie O'Halloran back?'

De Silva hoped Petrie's optimism as to his topographical knowledge wouldn't prove misguided, but putting that thought out of his mind, he considered the question. 'It would be easiest to head west towards Colombo, but I wouldn't like to rule anything out. They may decide to take a less obvious route to throw us off the scent.'

'In other words, we have a difficult task ahead of us,' said Archie glumly.

'I can't stay up here much longer,' said Petrie. 'There are matters I must deal with down in Kandy, but I'll see what I can do about sending you reinforcements. Are there roadblocks set up on the roads down to Kandy and Colombo?'

'Inspector Singh at Hatton has seen to that.'

'Good.'

'What if these men steer clear of roads?' asked Archie. 'I doubt the author of the threatening letters is a local, but if he's one of the kidnappers, as seems most likely, he may have hired guides to help them travel through the jungle and live off what they can forage.'

Archie had a point, thought de Silva. If the kidnappers had helpers well versed in forest craft, they might be able to survive for weeks, allowing them time to get away undetected. And hampered by their assurances to Hank O'Halloran, there was probably little he, Archie, and Petrie could do to stop them.

CHAPTER 7

At the police station the following morning, he tried to get on with some routine work, but concentration eluded him. It was impossible to get the case out of his mind.

'This morning seemed interminable,' he said when he returned home for lunch with Jane.

'What have you been doing?'

He grimaced. 'Nothing of any importance. Murdering time.'

'Killing time, dear.'

'Whichever it is, it was a pointless use of it.'

'I hope poor Mr O'Halloran gets his money without any difficulty,' said Jane frowning. 'And I hope he's approaching this the right way.'

Near the verandah where they sat drinking coffee after their meal, a thrush foraging among some dead leaves found a snail and proceeded to hammer it on a stone to break the shell. De Silva winced at the insistent noise; his nerves must be more on edge than he'd thought. He shrugged. 'He's convinced that the kidnappers mean business, and I have to admit, in his shoes, I wouldn't like to take any chances. I'm pinning my hopes on catching them after they give the lady up.'

'Will you go back to the police station this afternoon?'

'I'd better do to keep up morale. I can tell Prasanna and Nadar are disappointed not to be taking a more active part.'

He sighed. 'Although at the moment, I might say the same.'

It was late afternoon when he received a telephone call from Charlie Frobisher.

'All set for the morning, Inspector. O'Halloran has the money. The plan is for him to use the car he's borrowed from the Residence to drive to the shrine. If you'll bring your men, I'll drive the boss over.'

De Silva thanked him, but when he had put the telephone down, he felt uneasy. Frobisher's breezy tone had almost made it seem as if he was setting out the arrangements for a pleasant picnic, not an expedition that would decide the fate of a young lady whose life was in danger.

'I'm sure Charlie Frobisher is as concerned as you are,' said Jane when he mentioned the feeling to her that evening. 'It just isn't the British way to show it.'

'I suppose you're right.' He took a sip of the post-prandial whisky he had allowed himself. He didn't usually drink at this time of day, but he wanted something to steady his nerves. He was aware of being more rattled by this crime than most of the others he had been obliged to deal with, and he had a sneaking suspicion that it was because Marie O'Halloran had such exceptional beauty and charm. It was unfair that such people commanded more sympathy than those who were plain and gauche, but it was a fact of life. Marie possessed a magic that was hard to resist; if all she had done at Florence's party was read from the telephone directory, he believed she would still have held her audience in the palm of her hand.

At the outer limit of the light cast by the verandah's lamps, something small and dark scurried across the lawn and disappeared into the bushes. It didn't have the loping gait of a monkey, and other small animals like the civet tended to stay up in the trees.

'Did you see something?' he asked Jane.

She looked up from her embroidery. 'Where?'

'Over there – running into those bushes.' He scowled. 'Perhaps it was a squirrel. Maybe the same one that did the damage in my garden shed.' He realised that he had forgotten to mention it to Anif, but probably by now the gardener had found it for himself and cleared up.

He leant back in his chair, letting the throb of the cicadas soothe him as he and Jane fell into a companionable silence. Eventually, the chime of the clock in the drawing room striking eleven drifted out on the night air, and he yawned. 'I think I'll get ready for bed. It's an early start in the morning.'

Jane put down her embroidery; reaching for his hand, she gave it a squeeze.

'What's that for?'

'Everything will come right, dear. Try not to worry.'

'I hope so. I don't know why, but I have a bad feeling about this.'

'Any more so than with your other cases?'

'For some reason, yes.' He shrugged. 'Age creeping up on me, probably. People say one worries less, but I find the opposite. I've come to think youth has a natural optimism that fades as we grow older.'

'So, perception is subjective and has nothing to do with the outcome of events. Whatever is going to happen will happen, despite how each of us anticipates it. My prediction, for what it's worth, is that the kidnappers will take their money, and Mr O'Halloran will get his daughter back.'

De Silva laughed. 'You make it sound easy, my love. I'll tell myself that as I try to sleep.'

CHAPTER 8

Phoebe Tankerton planted her elbows on the dressing table in her bedroom at the Residence and stared at her reflection in the mirror. Her scowl deepened as she noticed that a new spot threatened to erupt on her chin. Oh, why was her nose too long and her hair so wild and all the wrong colour? She hated her red hair; she remembered all the occasions when the nannies employed to look after her by her mother had dragged the hairbrush through it, tearing out tangles and making her eyes water. They'd hated her, and she had hated them.

There was a knock at the door, and her mother's maid entered. 'Madam sent me to help you dress, Miss Phoebe,' she said hesitantly.

'Go back and tell her I'm not coming down to dinner. She'll have to make an excuse.'

'But, miss—'

Swinging around on the dressing table stool, Phoebe glowered, but her cheeks were wet.

The maid obviously felt a pang of sympathy for her. 'Very well, miss. I'll tell madam.'

As the door closed behind the maid, Phoebe turned back to the mirror. Her cheeks burned. She got up and went to the basin of washing water that the maid had left for her earlier. It had cooled and a layer of soapy scum had formed on the surface, but she dipped her hands in and pressed the palms to her cheeks to cool them. If Mother tried to insist on her coming down, she wouldn't give in.

She'd heard Hank O'Halloran was to dine in his room. Apparently, he'd left for Colombo long before dawn to collect this ransom money and was exhausted from the journey there and back. Without him or Marie present, dinner was bound to be a dreary affair. The Clutterbucks were so old and dull, and if they'd invited anyone else, they were bound to be old and dull too.

A tear slid down her cheek and plopped into the basin of water; she shivered. She missed Marie so much. No one like her had ever been kind before.

Despite the fact she was determined not to go to dinner, she went over to the wardrobe and opened it. That horrible electric-blue dress confronted her. When she'd persuaded her mother to buy it for her, she'd thought it so stylish, but catching a glimpse of herself in the long mirror at the top of the staircase on the evening of the party, she'd realised it was hideous. She scraped the hanger along the rail to push the dress out of the way.

Everything else in the cupboard was so childish: the muslins with their frills, and the velvets with their prissy little collars. It seemed longer than three days ago that Marie had laughed about how the dresses reminded her of the ones young ladies wore in Victorian picture books.

'All you need is a shovel-brimmed bonnet and a muff to look like one of those cute heroines Charles Dickens wrote about,' she'd teased. It had hurt a little, but then Maire must have noticed, for she'd promised to take Phoebe shopping with her when she visited London.

'Your mother won't mind,' she'd said cheerfully. 'And there are shops in Bond Street full of glamorous things you'll absolutely adore.'

'Well, I don't know—'

'Oh, don't be silly, darling. I'm sure your parents can

afford it. What's the use of having money if you never spend it? Pa never grudges a cent I spend on clothes.' Marie shrugged. 'I wouldn't stand for it if he did.'

They'd been sitting in Phoebe's room, Phoebe perched on the bed while Marie riffled through the clothes and shoes in the wardrobe. She turned and looked appraisingly at Phoebe. 'You have nice legs, so all these shoes must go. You need something to show them off. Anyway, you'll be doing the Season soon, won't you? You'll need the right clothes and accessories for that.'

The Season: a queasy feeling came over Phoebe when she thought of it. Young men with sweaty hands and braying laughs: how would she bear it? If only she had Marie to go to the dances with, but Marie would probably have gone home to America by then. Anyway, she said Americans didn't do the Season.

A cold hand closed around her heart and all thoughts of dresses and parties vanished. What if Marie came to harm? What if she never saw her again?

CHAPTER 9

De Silva parked the Morris a little way off the road at a place close enough to the shrine to hear O'Halloran when he called them – he'd been supplied for the purpose with a whistle that imitated a bird call and made a low, but penetrating sound – but not so close as to be seen if the kidnappers were watching. As he, Prasanna, and Nadar got out of the car, all dressed in plain clothes, O'Halloran swept past them. De Silva caught a glimpse of him in profile, rigidly upright with his body close to the steering wheel and his expression blank.

A few moments later, three cars drew up behind the Morris. One of them disgorged Charlie Frobisher and Archie Clutterbuck, the others, driven respectively by Andrew Patterson and one of the Residence's drivers, contained a group of servants from the Residence.

'It's not ideal,' said Archie, coming over to where de Silva stood with his men, 'but the best we could do in the circumstances. William Petrie has arranged for some of the Kandy force to watch the first villages that the kidnappers are likely to reach in all directions, but it will be hard for them to make an arrest without knowing exactly who they're looking for. The best scenario is that we catch up with them before then. You and I may not have much of a turn of speed, de Silva, but these young ones should have a better chance.'

Even speed might not be much use, thought de Silva gloomily. He knew from experience that it was very hard to find someone in the jungle if they didn't want to be found. Still, if they got Marie O'Halloran back, that would be a great achievement in itself. All the same, it still left them with the possibility that if the kidnappers were only after money, they might strike more than once, so extra vigilance would be needed. He was rather surprised that the Tankertons had let Patterson leave Phoebe's side again. Presumably, Archie had arranged for a good number of the Residence's security staff to be on duty.

Andrew Patterson wandered off to stand on his own. Dismissed by Archie, the Residence's servants settled themselves in the shade of a clump of banana trees. They were silent at first, but then started to talk quietly. Archie threw them an irritable glance. 'Go and tell them to stop, Frobisher,' he muttered. 'Sound carries, you know. We don't want to advertise our presence.'

Frobisher nodded and went over to the group of servants who quickly fell silent again.

Taking de Silva aside so that Prasanna and Nadar were out of earshot, Archie prodded the leaf litter with his stick. 'I hope to God we haven't made a mistake here, de Silva,' he said very quietly.

'If it's any consolation, sir, I don't think we had much choice.'

'I suppose not. But if this goes wrong, O'Halloran may try to pin the blame on us, even though we've only gone along with his wishes.'

De Silva wondered if his boss's assessment of the American stemmed from his behaviour in the present situation, or whether it dated from before it. Certainly, it was easy to believe that, despite the charm, O'Halloran might be a tough character to deal with. He was a strange mixture. De Silva remembered the genuine feeling he'd shown when

Marie laughed about the clairvoyant she and Phoebe had visited. He'd heard it said more than once that the Irish had a romantic streak and many of them remained very close to the myths and legends of their homeland. Perhaps O'Halloran's character was a classic example of a fusion of that streak with the practical, go-getter spirit he'd noticed in the Americans he'd come across in the course of his career.

'What do you make of that fellow Patterson?' muttered Archie, interrupting de Silva's thoughts.

'I'm not sure, sir. We've hardly spoken.'

Archie smiled dryly. 'I'll take that as ambivalence.'

De Silva examined his conscience. He couldn't deny that he wasn't impressed with Patterson. Granted, Marie O'Halloran hadn't been his responsibility, but where had he been at the Residence party? Was it really too much to expect of him to have followed Phoebe discreetly when she went upstairs with Marie? If he had, he might have heard the sounds of the scuffle Phoebe spoke of and been in time to avert catastrophe.

'O'Halloran's taking a long time,' said Archie, consulting his watch. He went over to Frobisher. 'I expected to hear the whistle by now. If the damn thing doesn't work, I'll have something to say about it.'

Charlie Frobisher, who had provided the whistle, looked uncomfortable.

Another ten minutes passed. 'Something's gone wrong. I'm sure of it,' growled Archie. He beckoned to the most senior of the servants and the man hurried over. 'The other men are to stay here, understand? None of them go anywhere until I give the order, but you come with me. If necessary, I'll send you back to fetch the rest.'

He nodded to de Silva and Frobisher. 'I want you with me. Bring your men, de Silva.' He glanced at Patterson as if he'd only just remembered he was there. 'Oh, and you too.'

Quietly, they set off in the direction of the shrine, keeping to the shelter of the trees. The heat had intensified in the time they had waited, and the jungle air dripped with humidity. Orchids sprouted from moss-covered branches and lianas snaked through the tangled vegetation. Sweat plastered de Silva's shirt to his back, and Archie's face was red and glistening, although neither Charlie Frobisher nor Patterson seemed to be as badly affected. Whatever one's opinion of Patterson, he wasn't out of condition, thought de Silva.

He cursed under his breath as he stepped on a small log hidden under the carpet of detritus on the ground. It rolled and his foot gave way, administering a sharp twist to his ankle. He bent down to rub it and hoped it wouldn't swell. Gingerly, he took the next step. He must keep up; the others were already a little way ahead.

It was then that he heard the shot.

* * *

By the time they had followed the kidnappers' instructions given to O'Halloran and fought their way along the overgrown path to the clearing where the handover was supposed to have taken place, they found only two people there: Hank O'Halloran and his daughter.

She lay not far from the path de Silva and Archie were on – the same one she and her father would most likely have returned by. O'Halloran was crouched on the dusty ground beside her, his arms wrapped around her limp body. The blood that soaked the back of her dress and turned her dark hair the colour of rust was on him too.

A stick cracked under Archie's foot, sounding like a thunderclap in the silence. O'Halloran's head jerked up, and he saw them. Even though de Silva was accustomed to witnessing tragedy, the misery in the man's eyes cut him to the heart.

'Good God, what's happened here?' asked Archie.

'She's dead. My girl's gone.'

'Are you hurt?'

O'Halloran shook his head. 'There were two of them. One was holding Marie at gunpoint. The other started checking the money in the bag.'

A deep crease appeared between his brows and his fists balled. 'I'll never forgive myself for making such a crass mistake. The bank had no used notes, so I agreed to them giving me new ones. The guy searching the bag got suspicious. He asked why I'd done that. The serial numbers were too easy to read. He started saying they were probably marked too. When I said no, he just sneered and told his partner to take Marie away. Then he shut the bag and started to make off into the jungle, calling the other guy to follow him.' He pointed in the direction.

'I saw red then. God knows what they'd have done with her.' O'Halloran wiped his eyes. 'She kept a more level head than I did. Before I had time to make a move, she broke away from the guy holding her and kicked him hard in the shins. He yelled and she shouted at me to run. I headed for the path I'd come in by, thinking she was behind me.'

He stopped, choked with emotion.

'Then I heard the shot. When I looked back, she was on the ground. The guy who'd been holding her had the gun in his hand, still smoking, and he was looking straight at me. I'll never know why he didn't pull the trigger again. He would have had a clear shot, but instead, he turned tail and ran off into the trees.'

'Panicked, I imagine,' said Archie sagely.

'Can you describe these men for us, sir?' asked de Silva.

O'Halloran had covered his face. His shoulders shook. Awkwardly, Archie put a hand on one of them. 'Just do your best, old man.'

When O'Halloran raised his head, his eyes were

red-rimmed and glistening with tears. 'I'm sorry, I know it's important, but I can't give you much to go on. They looked like locals. One guy, the one who did the talking, was much skinnier than the other. Both about the same height, a few inches shorter than you.' He looked at de Silva.

'What age?' asked Archie.

'Hard to say. All I can tell you is that they weren't young men.'

'How were they dressed?'

'Shabby brown trousers and vests. Apart from that—'

He knuckled more tears from his eyes. 'It was my fault. I shouldn't have run when she told me to. I should have gone for the guy with the gun and taken him down.'

'We all have our regrets,' said Archie. 'It's easy to make a mistake in the heat of the moment, and hindsight's a wonderful thing.'

'I guess so,' said O'Halloran but he didn't look comforted. His next words came out in a hoarse whisper. 'But if I hadn't run, she'd be alive now.'

Not for certain, thought de Silva. Both of them might have been shot. But O'Halloran was obviously in no mood to be consoled.

Glancing at Archie, de Silva saw that his boss was saying something to Charlie Frobisher. When he shifted his attention to de Silva, Archie shook his head almost imperceptibly. He was right; this wasn't the time to ask any more questions. O'Halloran needed to be in a calmer frame of mind.

'I think it's high time we got you back to the Residence, O'Halloran,' said Archie. 'Frobisher, may I use your car?'

'Certainly, sir.'

At first, de Silva thought the American would refuse to leave his daughter's body, but eventually, he stumbled to his feet. He seemed to have aged twenty years. Archie indicated the path back to the shrine. 'This way.'

As the two men disappeared into the trees, Charlie Frobisher came over to where de Silva stood. 'The poor fellow would do no good here,' he said. 'He's too distressed and who can blame him? The boss will send Hebden out to collect the body and take it back to town.' He looked closely at de Silva. 'What's on your mind?' he asked.

'I was just wondering if the kidnappers ever intended to release Marie O'Halloran.'

'Do you mean that the business about the money being suspicious may have been a ruse to avoid handing her over?' asked Frobisher, quickly following de Silva's train of thought.

'Perhaps. I've heard of cases where kidnappers feared a victim would identify them and used a bogus handover as a way of getting the money, while also disposing of the inconvenient witness to their crime.'

Frobisher groaned. 'If you're right, the poor girl never had a chance. A fact that probably won't be lost on her father when he's up to thinking more clearly.'

Prasanna and Nadar who had been waiting a little way off, uncomfortable witnesses to the tragedy, moved closer to Marie O'Halloran's body.

'What shall we do, sir?' asked Prasanna. De Silva wished he knew what was best. Before he could speak, Andrew Patterson intervened.

'Start in the direction O'Halloran showed us. We've already wasted too much time talking.'

Angry with himself, de Silva feared he had a point. Distracted by O'Halloran's plight, they had lost precious minutes.

'You—' Patterson jerked a thumb at Nadar. 'Go and get that bunch of servants moving. We need them here.'

Nadar, who didn't look very pleased at being addressed in such an offhand manner, and by a stranger, looked at de Silva, who nodded. He was irritated, but someone needed to wait with the body, and if Patterson wanted to take charge of the search, let him. De Silva wasn't convinced it would do any good. 'You may go too, Prasanna,' he said. 'I'll wait here until Doctor Hebden comes.'

'I'll come with you, Patterson,' said Charlie Frobisher.

Patterson put up a hand to shield his eyes from the sun. 'Right. We'd better get on with it.'

CHAPTER 10

Hebden put his black bag on the ground and hunkered down next to Marie's body. 'I don't know why I brought this,' he remarked gesturing to the bag. 'Habit, I suppose. There's no doubt the poor lady's dead.'

Carefully, he studied the situation. 'From the position of the entry wound, death was probably very swift, instantaneous even.'

He stood up, pulled out a handkerchief, and wiped his hands. 'What's the story? When Clutterbuck called me, we didn't talk for long. I understand he was anxious to keep an eye on O'Halloran in case he did anything foolish. Poor chap was very cut up, Clutterbuck said. Not surprisingly.'

He listened as de Silva went through O'Halloran's account and explained his and Frobisher's suspicion. When de Silva had finished, Hebden scratched his chin.

'Well, O'Halloran's lucky to be alive, although I don't suppose he'll see it that way. At any rate, not for a long time.'

'Quite; but I hope when he's calmer, he might remember something else about the encounter that will give us some clues.'

'Where have the rest of your party got to?'

'Searching for the kidnappers.'

Hebden raised an eyebrow. 'Good luck to them. Still, I suppose one has to try.'

'Before this happened, William Petrie had already arranged for some of the Kandy police to keep watch further out from here. Let's hope the kidnappers pass through a town or village eventually and are apprehended.'

'Are they likely to attract attention though?'

'If it's a small enough community they might. Although I admit we'll need luck to be on our side,' he added with a sigh.

Hebden scanned the area. 'Hmm. Nowhere safe to leave the body. I'll get a blanket from the car to cover it then drive back to Nuala and alert the undertakers. In the circumstances, I'm sure they'll come out straight away. Will you stay here until then, de Silva?'

'Of course. Patterson, appears to have taken charge of the search.'

Hebden gave him a wry look.

'I must admit, I find his attitude high-handed,' said de Silva. 'If he'd been doing his job properly, none of this might have happened.'

Hebden looked puzzled. 'But isn't he employed to protect the Tankertons' daughter?'

'Yes, but she went up to the bedroom at the same time as Marie O'Halloran.'

'Ah, I take your point, but in the chap's defence, he may have thought the Residence was a safe place.'

'I suppose that's true.'

After Hebden had brought the blanket to cover the body then left him, de Silva spent a while searching the clearing, paying particular attention to the places where O'Halloran had said that the kidnappers stood. It wasn't unknown for criminals to leave a clue behind. But the ground was dry and covered with a substantial layer of leaf litter. He wasn't surprised there were no discernible footprints.

He looked at his watch; the undertakers were taking their time. Idly, he poked with a stick at the dead leaves and rotting bark around the spot where the man who shot Marie had been.

Then his pulse quickened: bright against the drab colours of bark and leaves, he saw something white. He bent down to pick it up. It was a business card, and on it were printed the words *Andrew Patterson, Private Detective and Security Specialist*. A post restante address in England where mail could be sent followed.

Brushing flecks of dirt off the card, de Silva put it in his pocket. So, the man was of no fixed address. More importantly, why was the card there at all? He wouldn't challenge him yet, but he needed to find out more about Andrew Patterson.

CHAPTER 11

By the time the undertakers had removed Marie O'Halloran's body, there was still no sign of the searchers returning. There was little point trying to link up with them now, so de Silva decided to return to Nuala.

At Sunnybank, Jane greeted him solicitously. 'I've heard the news,' she said. 'How very sad. You must have had a dreadful morning.'

'Who told you?'

'Florence. She telephoned to say she was needed at the Residence and wouldn't be able to help me with the church flowers as we'd arranged. Luckily, Emerald stepped into the breach and gave me a lift to the church as well.'

She sighed. 'Florence told me that Mr O'Halloran is terribly distressed. I know it won't bring his daughter back, but do you think you've a chance of catching the kidnappers?'

'I'm not confident. They may have gone anywhere, and O'Halloran couldn't give us much of a description. Patterson and Frobisher are still out with Prasanna, Nadar and some of the Residence servants searching the area where she was found, but I'm not expecting it to be of much use.'

'Oh dear, poor Mr O'Halloran. Such a dreadful thing to happen. To lose one's child seems to go against the natural order of everything.'

'Indeed it does.' De Silva wiped his forehead. 'Is there anything to eat? I'm starving.'

'Of course, go and wash, and I'll have something brought for you.'

In the bathroom, he washed his hands and face and combed his hair. It still troubled him that he'd allowed the search to be delayed, even if it was only by a few minutes. Still, it was too late to do anything about it now, so there was no point tormenting himself. He hadn't been the only one to make the mistake. It occurred to him that Patterson had kept his distance while they had been listening to O'Halloran. Was there something to be read into the fact that he let time pass before he intervened?

Resolving to eat first and think later, he joined Jane in the dining room just as a servant was putting down a plate of omelette at the place laid for him. He hoped it would just be a starter. Omelette was something Jane had taught their cook to make. It was a French dish she had enjoyed when she lived in Paris for a few months with one of the families she had worked for before their marriage. It was pleasant enough, provided the eggs were lightly cooked and flavoured with green chillies and onions, but it was no substitute for proper food.

Jane must have divined his thoughts for she smiled. 'It's only to keep you going while the rest is prepared.'

'Good.'

'Emerald and I think that the Tankertons would leave Nuala if it wasn't for their concern for O'Halloran,' said Jane as he ate.

He swallowed a mouthful of egg and shrugged.

'What is it?'

'They may be safer staying at the Residence with extra people to protect them. I'm concerned about their security man, Patterson.'

'Really? Whatever for?'

She listened as he explained about the business card.

By the time he finished, her expression was thought-ful. 'So, the kidnappers may have been Patterson's men.

Travelling with the Tankertons, he would have had time to find out about Hank O'Halloran's wealth.' She frowned. 'But wouldn't Phoebe Tankerton be the greater prize? Perhaps she was his original target and the plan went wrong. The men who acted as his accomplices may have snatched the wrong girl.'

De Silva shook his head. 'As the kidnappers were waiting on the balcony outside Marie's room rather than Phoebe's, I doubt it.'

'True, and I suppose Phoebe would be a more challeng-ing target. Even with Patterson guarding her, her parents rarely let her out of their sight. If he is behind this, it must be frustrating for him that he lost an opportunity to capture Phoebe instead of Marie.'

De Silva remembered Phoebe saying that Patterson had let her go upstairs at the ball with Marie as she was a friend. Had he seen a chance and hoped his men would seize it and take both girls? It would have been a daring move and unlikely unless he had tipped them off in advance that it was worth kidnapping Phoebe, but if that was his intention, they had failed him.

Jane rested her chin on her cupped hand. 'I wonder what went wrong. The kidnappers had their money. Why not give Marie back as they'd promised?'

'Hard to say.' De Silva forked up the last of the omelette. 'O'Halloran said they were suspicious about the money, but Charlie Frobisher and I wonder if that was a ruse.'

'You mean to avoid handing Marie over?'

He nodded.

'Or they genuinely feared a trap and panicked,' added Jane.

'Maybe. Where guns are concerned, matters often quickly get out of hand. Nonetheless, unless the searchers find the money, it looks like the kidnappers still took it.'

The rest of the meal arrived. Pleased to see it included a

creamy curry made with tomatoes, onions, and some of his new beetroots, he turned his attention to doing it justice. No one should be expected to think too deeply on an empty stomach.

'Shall I order some tea for you?' asked Jane when he'd finished.

He shook his head. 'Thank you, but no. I'd better get up to the Residence and see what's going on there.'

Coming around to her side of the table, he dropped a kiss on her head. 'I'll try not to be too late home.'

Outside, he headed for the Morris. He had parked it in the shade of a clump of trees, although now it was hardly necessary as the sun had moved round. As he neared the car, a dark shape scuttled out from behind a wheel. It appeared to split into two before it vanished.

De Silva blinked. The late afternoon light had a way of making things hazy. His eyes were probably playing tricks.

CHAPTER 12

By the time he reached the Residence, darkness had fall-en. In Archie Clutterbuck's study, he found his boss in a gloomy mood. 'Well, de Silva,' he said wearily. 'We have an utter disaster on our hands, and I hear that you and Frobisher think we may never have stood a chance of res-cuing the girl anyway. So, what do you suggest we do now?' He laced his hands together and flexed them; the knuckles cracked. 'I don't see what else we could have done, what with O'Halloran insisting we stay in the background, but if he changes his tune now, there'll be hell to pay.'

'I think I may have something, sir.'

'Do you?' Archie sighed. 'We can't bring the poor girl back, but I suppose it would be a small consolation if we manage to apprehend the culprits and recover O'Halloran's money.'

He listened carefully, for once without interrupting, while de Silva explained about the business card and his thoughts on Andrew Patterson.

'It's plausible.'

Pressing the tips of his fingers together, Archie sat back in his chair and regarded de Silva pensively. 'I agree that we definitely need to know more about the man. All we have at the moment is what Tankerton told me about his references being satisfactory. I think a call to Scotland Yard is in order. Will you leave that with me, de Silva?'

'Of course, sir.'

'Hopefully, they'll be able to come up with something in a couple of days. Meanwhile, I don't think we should alert the Tankertons. We might be wrong about Patterson, and I don't want another mistake. But I'll put young Frobisher in the picture, and my people can carry on keeping a close eye on Phoebe, so she'll be perfectly safe. Do you agree?'

De Silva nodded, slightly surprised by the tone of the question. Archie really was mellowing. 'On the other hand, sir, if Patterson is our man, we don't want him giving us the slip. May I suggest I send my sergeant and my constable up to the Residence? If we disguise them as servants, they can keep an eye on him unobserved.'

'Hmm. Not a bad idea. I'll ask my wife to see to it that they're suitably kitted out.'

There was a knock at the door. Archie called out and Florence came in.

'Ah, my dear, you've arrived at an opportune moment.'

While Archie explained about Andrew Patterson and the plan to put Prasanna and Nadar on duty at the Residence, de Silva watched Florence's little black and white household mop of a dog, Angel, strut over to Darcy, the Labrador, who was lying in his usual place beside his master's chair. At Angel's approach, Darcy rolled on his back and thumped his tail. Like his master, he obviously knew who was boss, thought de Silva.

'How dreadful,' said Florence when Archie came to the end of the story. 'And the Tankertons have trusted him with their daughter. It's shocking how wicked some people are.'

'We mustn't prejudge, my dear,' said Archie mildly. 'Patterson may be as innocent as the day is long. The inspector and I have merely agreed that we need to find out more about him.'

Florence sniffed. 'The evidence sounds compelling to me, but you must go about these things in your own way.'

Archie smiled ruefully as she left the study, Angel trotting at her heels. 'If Mrs Clutterbuck was to be appointed to the bench, I think the accused would approach her in fear and trembling. But in her defence, she's very upset by what's happened. In a short space of time, Hank O'Halloran has made many friends here, as had his daughter. It will be a terrible blow to the Tankertons if we find out that it was the very man that they brought in to protect their own daughter who orchestrated this appalling crime.'

'How is Mr O'Halloran bearing up?'

'A shadow of his former self. Pitiable to witness.' Archie hauled himself out of his chair. 'It's time I went up to dress for dinner, although for once, I don't find the idea of food very appealing. I'll walk to the hall with you, de Silva.'

In the reception hall, they met Andrew Patterson coming in from the drive.

'Ah, Patterson,' said Archie, with an admirable lack of embarrassment. 'What news? I fear from your expression that it's not good.'

'It's not, I'm afraid,' said Patterson casting de Silva a sour glance. 'It's grown too dark to see, but we'll start again at first light.'

'Hold your horses for now. We'll consider the situation tomorrow and decide what's best.'

Patterson looked as if he was going to argue but had then thought better of it.

'Is Charlie Frobisher with you?' asked Archie.

'I expect he's somewhere about. He set off a little ahead of me. Your servants should all be back here by now.'

He made no mention of Prasanna and Nadar, nor did Archie, and de Silva decided not to draw attention to them. It was a good thing if Patterson had hardly noticed them during the search, although hopefully, they hadn't had to walk all the way back to town.

'I'll say goodnight, de Silva,' said Archie. 'We'll speak tomorrow.'

'Thank you, sir.'

Was he imagining it, wondered de Silva, or did Andrew Patterson's eyes bore into his retreating back as he went out of the front door and down the steps? Was the fellow genuinely putting the blame for losing the kidnappers on him, or did it just suit him to do so?

* * *

The lights were out at the police station and the door locked. In case Prasanna and Nadar were already home, before setting off in the direction of the shrine to see if they needed rescuing, de Silva drove through town to the area where they lived.

In contrast to the spacious bungalows and gardens where the British community and the better-off locals had their residences, the place was a warren of houses crowded close together, in many places so close that the inhabitants had strung their washing lines from one side of the street to the other. Like bunting at festival time, clothes flapped gently in the evening breeze. Although the streets were rough, unpaved, and lacking street lighting, there was very little rubbish to be seen. This was not one of the poorest areas of town, reflected de Silva. Most families living here had food to eat and clothes to wear. The children running around and playing looked well fed.

He came to Sergeant Prasanna's home first – part of a large, dilapidated house. The communal yard and entrance he went in by were, however, clean. As he climbed the two flights of stairs to Prasanna's front door, there was a pleasing smell of simmering curry and baking bread. He knocked and the door was opened by Prasanna's wife, Kuveni. Her face broke into a happy smile, and she put the palms of her hands together and made a little bow.

'Inspector de Silva! We are honoured.'

De Silva reached out and patted her cheek. He and Jane had become very fond of Kuveni when she'd lived with them for a few months before her marriage to Sergeant Prasanna. 'No need for formality, my dear. I trust you and your daughter are well?'

'Very well, thank you.'

'Is that rascal of a husband of yours at home? If he is, I'd like a word with him.'

Kuveni stood aside, and de Silva saw a bare-footed Prasanna, dressed only in a white dhoti, coming out of the kitchen with the baby in his arms. He noted that she was blessed with her parents' good looks. Prasanna would have to be a vigilant father when she grew into a young lady.

But at the moment, he looked worried. 'Inspector, sir. I hope you don't mind. Mr Frobisher offered to drive Nadar and me back to Nuala. There was no sign of you at the station, so we came home.'

Ah, so Charlie Frobisher had done the decent thing. He could always be relied on, but it must have been a squash in that sporty car of his.

'I haven't come to drag you back to the station,' de Silva said with a smile. 'But I'm afraid I am going to disturb your evening for a little while, because I have an important job for you and Nadar in the morning. Let's walk round to his house, and I'll tell you all about it there.'

While Prasanna went to find a shirt and some shoes, de Silva chatted to Kuveni.

'My husband has told me about the poor lady who was killed, sir,' she said, her brown eyes full of pity. 'It will be a great sorrow for her father.'

De Silva thought how much more strongly such a loss was bound to resonate with those who had children of their own than with those who did not.

'I hope you will catch the man soon,' Kuveni went on.

'I hope so too. And with your husband's help,' he added kindly, 'I'm sure we will.'

'Thank you, sir. He is very keen to do well. I'm glad you are pleased with his work.'

De Silva smiled at the pride in her eyes.

Prasanna reappeared, dressed and ready to go, and they set off. Nadar's home was only a few minutes' walk away. It was very similar to Prasanna's but smaller, and fuller too with a baby and a little boy in the family. Nadar's wife, whom de Silva had met on only a handful of occasions, gave him a respectful greeting then disappeared, murmuring something about attending to the children, whilst he and Prasanna followed Nadar into a small living room. It was sparsely furnished, but a bright cotton rug and some children's toys gave it a cheerful air. De Silva sat down on one of the plump floor cushions and picked up a beautifully carved toy elephant that lay nearby.

'I think I recognise this. Your own handiwork?'

Nadar grinned sheepishly. 'Yes, sir. But now I only make them at home.'

De Silva remembered times past when he had spotted Nadar at work on a toy when he was supposed to be on duty. Time and family responsibilities had certainly bucked up his keenness to work hard. He nodded. 'I'm glad to hear it. Now, as I told Prasanna, tomorrow, I have an important job for you both.'

As he explained about Andrew Patterson and the plan to infiltrate them into the Residence, he noticed a gleam in the young men's eyes. No doubt, they would enjoy this bit of undercover work. 'You'll need to be careful,' he finished. 'Do you think Patterson got a good look at you during the search? If so, we'll have to consider more of a disguise than just the Residence's uniforms.'

Prasanna answered first.

'I don't think so, sir. He gave a lot of orders but never looked at our faces or asked us any questions.'

It was said without obvious rancour. Perhaps a young man like Prasanna was less easily offended than a middle-aged detective, thought de Silva. He reminded himself that in any case, it was fortunate that, for once, the tendency of some Britishers to be unable to distinguish one brown face from another, or even take the trouble to try, was going to work in their favour.

Their plans concluded, he walked back with Prasanna and returned to the Morris.

At home, there was no sign of Jane. 'The memsahib went out with Memsahib Hebden, sahib,' the servant said when he asked where she was. 'She left instructions for dinner, sahib. When will you be ready to eat it?'

'As soon as it's ready.'

The servant waggled his head. 'I will tell the cook straight away, sahib.'

That evening, a solitary meal proved not to be the best way of ending his day. Without Jane to talk to, his mind dwelt on Andrew Patterson to an extent that it might not have done if she had been there with her brisk brand of sympathy and advice.

When he had eaten his fill, de Silva poured himself a post-prandial whisky, put a record on the gramophone and went to sit on the verandah. It was foolish to let Patterson annoy him. The man might not be in Nuala much longer anyway. Even if he wasn't their quarry, he would leave when his employers moved on. He wondered whether, illogical as it might seem, his irritation with Patterson had something to do with Archie's mellowing. Was it a reminder that you won over one Britisher only to come up against another challenge?

Deep in thought, and the storm-laden music of Rachmaninoff's Second Piano Concerto, he didn't hear Jane return. As the last notes died away, she stepped out onto the verandah and put a hand on his shoulder making him start.

'I'm sorry I wasn't here when you came home, dear. Emerald telephoned. She and Doctor Hebden had been going to see the new film at the Casino, but he had to go out to visit a patient who was suddenly taken ill. Normally, I doubt she would mind, but she seemed so downcast tonight that I agreed to go with her.'

'Why tonight?' asked de Silva, a little irritably.

'I think this sad business with the O'Hallorans reminds her too much of the past.'

De Silva felt remorseful. Emerald was happily married now, but she had suffered her own family tragedy. 'Of course. I hadn't looked at it that way.' He took her hand. 'We're lucky never to have had to face anything like it ourselves.'

'Yes.'

She smiled and gestured in the direction of the gramophone. 'Rachmaninoff? Has there been a dramatic development in the case that I should know about?'

'Not in the way of solving it, I fear.'

He told her about his talk with Archie, the plan for Prasanna and Nadar, and his encounter with Patterson. 'Still,' he added, 'not all the British are such a confounded nuisance. Charlie Frobisher, for example, and even the Petries, despite their exalted position, are an entirely different kettle of worms.'

'Kettle of fish, dear. It's a can of worms.'

He shrugged. 'A kettle or a can, as long as I don't have to put up with Andrew Patterson for much longer, I'll be a happy man.'

'If he is your man, do you think he'll give himself away?'

'I doubt it will be easy to catch him out, but if he is the culprit, then we must. Others could be at risk. I'm looking forward to finding out what Scotland Yard have to say about him.'

CHAPTER 13

'I think I should speak to Phoebe Tankerton again,' he said at breakfast the following morning.

'Do you really think now is the right time?' asked Jane. 'Her parents won't want her upset.'

'Naturally. I'll have to be careful to reassure them that it's the last thing anybody wants.'

Strolling out to the Morris, he breathed in the morning air. The sky was a limpid blue. He had heard rain drumming on the roof overnight, and it had freshened the trees and plants.

As he drove up to the Residence, he noticed a small group of gardeners at work. He didn't like to stare too hard, but he was sure that one of them had the chunky build of Constable Nadar.

Walter and Grace Tankerton met him in the drawing room. They greeted him civilly enough, but he sensed they were wary. He made his request, but for a few moments, neither of them answered. Eventually, with a glance at his wife, it was Walter Tankerton who spoke.

'Inspector de Silva, my wife and I are very concerned for our daughter. She's taken this hard. I appreciate that you're happy for us to be present, but we must also have your assurance that if she becomes upset, the interview terminates immediately.'

'Of course, sir.'

Walter glanced at his wife once more. 'Gracie? What do you say?'

There were shadows under Grace Tankerton's eyes. 'I know it's for the best. I wouldn't want anyone else to suffer at the hands of these evil men.'

The thought that she and her family might be amongst those people was unspoken, but it hung in the air. She drew a shuddering breath. 'Oh, how much I wish this had never happened. Our poor girl was so fond of Marie. Phoebe has never found it easy to make friends, Inspector. Perhaps it's our fault; maybe we've been too protective of her. One tries to do the best for one's children, but it can be hard to know what that is. Sometimes, I feel that we and Phoebe live in different worlds.'

Her husband raised a hand. 'Gracie, try not to distress yourself. We've been over and over this.'

'Listen to me,' she said sadly. 'Feeling sorry for myself when poor Hank O'Halloran—'

'Enough, my dear,' said Walter quietly.

De Silva saw how deeply they both loved their daughter. It was sad that they obviously found it hard to get close to her. Jane had made a good point when she said Marie must have provided a welcome diversion from a life circumscribed by wealth, but it was a great shame if her company had also provided an escape from an unhappy family life that allowed her to avoid addressing the problem.

A servant was sent to fetch Phoebe. When she joined them, de Silva noticed that any vestige of self-confidence that she might have had was gone; she was an unhappy, frightened child. Her mother was right. Phoebe's distress at Marie's fate went deep. Was it also at the back of her mind that she too might be at risk unless the kidnappers were found?

After he had thanked her for seeing him, he asked her to tell him as much as she could remember of the events in the days leading up to the kidnap. Did she recall anything unusual? Had Marie mentioned noticing anyone following her? Did she seem anxious in any way?

To all of the questions, Phoebe shook her head.

'There was nothing like that. We talked as we always did. Recently, Marie was full of plans for when she and her father went back to America.' A wistful expression came into her eyes. 'She wanted me to come and visit her.' For a moment, bitterness replaced sorrow as she glanced at her mother. 'But I won't be going now.'

Grace looked away. De Silva felt a stab of pity for her. The tragedy hadn't been her fault.

'Mr O'Halloran mentioned that he had received threatening letters while you were all still in India,' said de Silva. 'I believe he dismissed them as unimportant, but do you have any idea if Marie was aware of them?'

Phoebe shook her head. 'She never mentioned anything like that.'

Grace Tankerton gave a sharp intake of breath and her husband's face darkened. 'Why weren't we informed of these letters?' he snapped.

De Silva took a deep breath. 'At the time when Mr O'Halloran revealed their existence to me, sir, there was no indication they posed a threat to anyone else. It's still not clear that they do.'

Walter Tankerton grunted. 'I take your point, but mine stands. Whatever the situation, I prefer to be in possession of all the facts.'

Uncomfortably, de Silva thought how another fact was being kept from him – the suspicion about Patterson. He hoped that wouldn't turn out to be a mistake.

Phoebe half rose from her chair. 'I'd like to go now. I haven't anything more to tell you.'

Grace Tankerton stood up too. 'I'll come with you, my dear. Perhaps you'd like a walk in the garden? I'm sure Patterson will accompany us.'

Phoebe scowled. 'No, I want to go to my room. Alone.'

At the sight of Grace Tankerton's defeated expression, de Silva felt a fresh stab of pity.

As he left the Residence, he continued to feel troubled by the question of whether the Tankertons should be told about Patterson. It was something he would need to discuss with Archie. Talk of the letters also reminded him that he hadn't yet spoken to O'Halloran's secretary.

'Good morning, Inspector!'

He looked up to see Charlie Frobisher coming across the drive. He wondered whether to mention Patterson but decided it was best to leave it to Archie to do that. He did, however, mention O'Halloran's secretary.

'It's tricky getting to talk to O'Halloran at the moment, as I'm sure you understand,' said Frobisher. 'But leave it with me. I'll see what I can do and telephone you.'

De Silva thanked him and went on his way.

CHAPTER 14

Frobisher's call came that afternoon as de Silva sat in his office at the police station, debating whether to telephone Archie and discuss what to do about Patterson and the Tankertons. He was close to reaching the conclusion that it would be best to try and persuade Archie to give them the information, rather than risk Walter Tankerton's wrath if the truth came to light in some other way.

'I managed to have a word with O'Halloran,' said Frobisher. 'He says by all means talk to his secretary. You'll find her at the Crown. Godley's her name: Miss Laura Godley. He doubts she'll give you anything useful, but in my opinion, as in yours, I think it's worthwhile. A good questioner can sometimes jog a memory that someone didn't know they had.'

'I hope it will prove so in this case.'

'O'Halloran was concerned that the lady's largely been left to fend for herself since he and his daughter moved to the Residence, and even more so now. Will you pass on his apologies and tell her that if there's anything she needs she only has to speak to the hotel management? You might have a word with them and say that O'Halloran authorises the hotel to give her whatever she asks for.'

'I'll do that and thank you for your help.'

'By the way,' added Frobisher. 'The boss has told me about Patterson.'

'Good.'

* * *

Laura Godley was of above average height for a woman. De Silva wouldn't have described her as pretty, but she was striking. He estimated that she was in her early forties. She wore a smart, cream linen dress, neatly belted at the waist, that gave her a business-like air. Her dark hair was caught up at the nape of her neck in a bun, and she wore a gold chain from which hung an oval medallion delicately engraved with the letters *L G*.

'Thank you for agreeing to talk with me, ma'am,' he said when, introductions over, they settled themselves in a small room off the lobby where de Silva's friend, Sanjeewa, had assured him that they would be undisturbed.

'It's no problem, Inspector.' Laura Godley's American accent was softer and more cultured than her boss's expansive twang. 'I'll be glad to help in any way that I can. But first, tell me how Hank's doing.'

Interesting that she used her boss's first name. Another example of American informality, perhaps. De Silva found it impossible to imagine Walter Tankerton's staff addressing him in such a fashion, or Archie's, for that matter.

'I'd not heard from him for a couple of days,' she went on. 'When Mr Frobisher telephoned from the Residence with this terrible news, I understood why. As I'm sure you'll understand, I don't want to bother him with business matters at a time like this. Luckily, nothing's come up except routine work that I usually deal with on my own initiative anyway.'

'I've seen very little of Mr O'Halloran myself, but I believe he's coping as well as one would expect in this sad situation. He sends you his good wishes and his apologies for the fact that you've been left to yourself for some time. If there's anything you need, you only have to ask, and I'm to inform the hotel management of that.'

Laura smiled. 'How like him to think of others, even at a time like this.'

'Have you worked for Mr O'Halloran for long, ma'am?'

'About five years, and I couldn't ask for a better boss. Prior to this, I worked for a large insurance company in New York. This way, I get the chance to travel and the job is always stimulating.' She sighed. 'I have no idea what will happen now with Marie gone. Hank will have to pick up the reins again eventually, but it will be hard, I'm sure of that.'

'What is the nature of Mr O'Halloran's business, if I may ask?'

'Oil mainly, and some interests in the metals' markets.'

It sounded suitably profitable.

'Forgive me, Inspector, I forgot to ask if you'd like me to order us some tea.'

'No thank you, ma'am, but please don't let me stop you.'

She reached out to straighten the pile of magazines that lay on the low table in front of her. He noticed that her hand trembled slightly; her poise was not as steady as one might have thought on first meeting her. She saw him looking and smiled awkwardly. 'But I'm sure you didn't come here to talk about me, or my career. Shall we get to the point?'

Briefly, de Silva went over most of the ground that he had with Phoebe Tankerton, allowing for the difference that Laura Godley was Hank's secretary, not Marie's friend. Taking that into account, the answers to his questions were much the same, so he soon moved on to the topic of the letters.

'There were four of them, at least that I saw,' said Laura. 'Two waiting for us in Delhi, one in Bombay, and the last one in Calcutta. None of them were handwritten.'

'Is it your guess they were all from the same person?'

'From the manner in which the writer expressed him or herself, I would say they were. They were signed off in the same way each time; every letter simply ended with the words "from a friend".'

'Can you remember anything that might help us track down the writer?'

She thought for a while before speaking. 'I'm sorry, there's nothing.'

'I imagine that you know Mr O'Halloran pretty well by now. Despite what he said about dismissing these letters, do you think that, in reality, he was rattled by them but didn't want to admit it?'

She shook her head emphatically. 'Not in the slightest. On every occasion, he laughed and said he wasn't going to waste his time worrying about crazy people, and I believe he meant it. I was to tear the letters up and we'd forget about them. So, that's exactly what I did, and I thought I was doing the right thing. Until now,' she added sadly. 'Inspector, do you believe someone has followed us from India? It's so horrible to think that we might have been spied on all that time, and now here—' She put her head in her hands for a moment, then looked back up. 'I'm sorry, Inspector. I was determined not to be foolish. Hank needs support, not theatricals.'

Awkwardly, de Silva searched for something consoling to say. It was hard to think of the right words given that he'd met Laura Godley less than an hour ago. In any case, his initial impression had been of someone who prided herself on her self-control, so she might not welcome words of comfort from a stranger.

She drew a deep breath. 'Well, that's about all I have to tell you, Inspector. Have you any other questions for me?'

'A last one, if I may. I'd be interested to know your opinion of Andrew Patterson.'

'The Tankertons' bodyguard? They call him a secretary, but a bodyguard's what we'd call him back home. I've had very little to do with him. Hank did mention on one occasion that he suspected Walter and Grace Tankerton placed a rather higher value on his services than they merited, but he didn't think it was up to him to interfere unless they asked his views.'

She looked at de Silva closely, and her eyes narrowed. 'Do you have something on him? If he has anything to do with this, the Tankertons will be devastated.'

'For the moment, I'd be grateful if you wouldn't mention that I asked you, ma'am. It's merely a routine enquiry. I understand Mr Patterson has very good references.'

'So I believe.' She uncrossed her legs and shifted to the edge of her chair. 'If there's nothing else I can help you with, I think I'll go to my room and rest. I haven't slept well the last few nights.'

De Silva noticed the shadows around her eyes and felt guilty. 'I'm sorry to have kept you, ma'am.'

'There's no need to apologise.'

* * *

After he and Laura Godley parted company, de Silva returned to the lobby and asked one of the receptionists to call through to Sanjeewa to see if he would spare him a few moments. While he waited for a reply, it occurred to de Silva that Laura Godley had never actually voiced her own opinion on Andrew Patterson, only her employer's. She was clearly an astute woman; de Silva wondered if she was suspicious of Patterson too. He filed that thought in his memory as he was shown to Sanjeewa's office.

Sun streamed through the windows lighting up his friend's chubby face. Sanjeewa stood up and shook his hand.

'How is the case going, my friend? I hope you learnt something useful from Miss Godley. She seems a very capable lady. Attractive too. I am surprised that she is still a secretary, not a wife.'

'You are behind the times, Sanjeewa.'

'Probably.' His friend grinned.

'In any case, the purpose of my visit is to tell you that Mr O'Halloran says she is to have whatever she needs while she is here. No expense spared.'

Sanjeewa raised an eyebrow. 'Perhaps she is wise to remain a secretary after all.'

CHAPTER 15

He stopped on the way back to the station to buy himself something to eat. After hastily consuming the bowl of string hoppers flavoured with sambols made of coconut, and caramelised onions and red chillies, he returned to the Morris.

Back at the station, there was no sign of Prasanna or Nadar. He assumed they were still carrying out their work at the Residence. A small heap of afternoon post lying just inside the door included a note from Archie asking him to come up there as soon as he returned. It was lucky he'd stopped for lunch.

'Awkward situation we've got here, de Silva,' said his boss when he was shown into the study. 'Hank O'Halloran's got it into his head that he wants to visit that fortune teller woman Phoebe Tankerton and his daughter went to see.'

De Silva recalled the conversation about the clairvoyant at the party to raise funds for the orphanage.

'Apparently, this woman also claims to be a medium and have the ability to talk to the dead. O'Halloran's set on getting her to contact Marie for him.'

De Silva frowned. He wondered if it was Marie who had told her father that the clairvoyant also claimed to be a medium. From the conversation at the party at the Residence, he'd had the impression that Marie had looked on her and Phoebe's visit to the clairvoyant as a piece of fun. He suspected she would have thought a visit to a medium would just be a spookier version of that. But he recalled that O'Halloran had taken his daughter to task for her frivolous attitude, and it was understandable that now, he would clutch at any straw. However, if he thought they would find and convict the criminals with the testimony of a woman speaking from the dead, he was headed for disappointment. It was an unorthodox method that would never stand up in court.

'Dubious business if you ask me.' Archie looked closely at de Silva. 'If you're thinking as I did when I first heard about it, that he hopes we'll nail the criminals that way, I believe you're on the wrong track. Once I'd talked to him for longer, I realised that what he really wants to know is that Marie is safe and forgives him. The poor fellow's still suffering from a powerful sense of guilt.'

He sighed. 'I suppose it will do no harm to humour him. I only hope this woman gives him a modicum of comfort, even if she's a charlatan after money. One wonders what she told O'Halloran's daughter about her fortune.'

It was an interesting point. Certainly, Marie O'Halloran hadn't seemed afraid of what she'd been told. Presumably, that meant the clairvoyant had predicted good fortune. If so, whether or not she was a fake, was that her stock performance to please clients and ensure they paid well?

Archie wiped his forehead with his handkerchief. 'I must admit, it's a turn of events that's surprised me. I hadn't expected anything quite like this from O'Halloran.' He grunted. 'Mumbo-jumbo to me, but we all have our foibles.'

'I remember, sir, at your party at the Residence, he spoke up for a clairvoyant who had predicted his family's future in America.'

Archie lit a cigarette, adding to the cirrus cloud of smoke above his head, and thought for a few moments. 'I'm sure I recall that he objected to his daughter and Phoebe going to see this woman,' he said at last.

'Only because he was concerned about the neighbourhood from a safety point of view.'

'Ah.' Archie rasped a hand over his chin. With everything that was going on, de Silva suspected he had forgotten to shave that morning. 'A man like O'Halloran's bound to dig his heels in if opposed,' Archie went on. 'On balance, there may not be much point trying to talk him out of the idea. If comfort comes at a price, so be it. Let's hope it's a reasonable one. Phoebe Tankerton's determined to go with him, and the Tankertons are wavering over whether to let her. Certainly, Mrs Tankerton's not keen to visit a second time. She described the house as a seedy old place. None of us know much about this woman, apart from what Marie and Phoebe mentioned at the party.'

'How did Miss O'Halloran come to hear of her in the first place, sir?'

Archie frowned. 'I can't recall... Ah yes, something about a conversation with a person she met in Calcutta. They asked where the O'Hallorans would be going in Ceylon, and when she mentioned Nuala, they waxed lyrical about this woman and explained where she was to be found.'

He paused a moment. 'Odd story, but then she was an unconventional young woman. Of course, if they do go, Andrew Patterson will accompany them as he did the first time. It's far too early to voice our suspicions about him, but in view of what you and I've discussed, I'd like there to be additional protection. In other words, you and your men, de Silva. Grace Tankerton ought to be reassured if you're there.'

'Of course, sir. When is Mr O'Halloran talking of going?'

'Tomorrow. I believe he was going to contact that secretary of his to arrange it.'

'I spoke to her this earlier this afternoon, but she didn't mention it.'

'Probably O'Halloran hadn't called her by then. Did she have anything useful to impart?'

'Unfortunately not, but she was insistent that O'Halloran hadn't been alarmed by the threatening letters.'

'Right. Well, I'll speak to the Tankertons. If they decide to agree, I'll get them to inform Patterson and pave the way with O'Halloran. The place is on the other side of town on Ridgeway Road. I expect O'Halloran will understand the Tankertons' reservations about letting Phoebe go without extra protection. But if he'd rather not advertise a police presence, you'd better go in plain clothes.'

He shrugged. 'As for Patterson, if he doesn't like it, he'll just have to bite his tongue or argue it out with them. Best that we don't get involved.'

'Speaking of Mr Patterson, sir, I'm uneasy about keeping our suspicions about him from his employers for too much longer.'

'If you're worried about the girl's safety, de Silva, set your mind at rest. She's safe in the Residence and there'll be plenty of people other than Patterson with her on this wretched outing. Even the most hardened criminal wouldn't take the risk of trying anything. Give it a few more days until we've heard from Scotland Yard.'

'Very well, sir.'

* * *

Once he had made the arrangements for Prasanna and Nadar to be released the following morning from their duties at the Residence in time to go to the police station to meet him, de Silva went back to the station. He glanced at the letters that he had thrown onto the counter in the public room before he set off to see Archie. He may as well go through them now.

A few minutes sufficed. He stretched his arms above his head and debated what to do next. It was tempting to call it a day and go home, but perhaps he would drive over to Ridgeway Road first. There was probably nothing to worry about, but he would like to get a feel for the place before tomorrow's event. It was always good to be aware of what you were dealing with. He liked to avoid nasty surprises whenever possible.

Despite O'Halloran's and Grace Tankerton's views, Ridgeway Road seemed to de Silva to be a reasonably respectable place. It was not one that he had often needed to visit, so he saw it with fresh eyes. Most of the buildings that flanked the wide roadway had columns or pillars that supported overhanging upper floors, so that the ground floor rooms benefited from the shade of loggias. In many cases, the facades were painted in red, sky blue, pale green, or mustard yellow, and the architecture had a Dutch flavour to it. He recalled this was the main part of Nuala where the influence of the Dutch, who had colonised his island before the British came, persisted, although in Colombo, there had been many more instances. He wondered what the road had been called in the time of the Dutch. Not Ridgeway Road, certainly.

Walking along the pavement, he saw that the shops occupying most of the ground floors were well stocked with all kinds of goods, from hardware and haberdashery to cheap jewellery and clothes. There were also several selling medical remedies, as well as a barber's shop, and a dentist whose window displayed a macabre range of false teeth. In one place, where a lane led off the road, there was a fruit and vegetable market where the stallholders were starting to close up for the day. Part of the market was covered by a broad archway that spanned the gap between the houses on either side.

The house that Archie had given him the number of was on the corner of the main road and this lane. Standing three storeys high, it had no loggia or shops on the ground floor. Instead, there were windows that were protected, like those above them, by metal grilles. The front door looked solid enough, but sun had bleached out most of its paint; indeed, the whole building looked to be in serious need of repair. De Silva assumed it was all residential. Patterson, who had, of course, been there before, had told Archie that from what he'd seen, the building looked to have been divided up for use as a lodging house at some time, and the medium's room was on the top floor at the front of the building. The building was mirrored by the one on the other side of the lane.

Under the cover of browsing his way along what was left on the market stalls, de Silva checked the windows on the side of the house: more metal grilles. The end of the lane was blocked off by high gates that looked as if they hadn't been opened for a long time.

Walking back towards Ridgeway Road, de Silva spoke to a few of the stallholders who were still there, claiming he was looking for a fortune teller who lived nearby and had been recommended to him, but no one had heard of one. He wasn't particularly surprised in such a busy area. Clearly, she didn't advertise her services with any posters or signs. It did surprise him, however, that some people claimed that the building had not been occupied for years.

As he emerged from the market lane, he noticed the remains of gateposts fixed to the walls on either side of him; the front of the lane might once have been gated as the rear was now. Perhaps at some time in the past, it had been used as a safe place to keep vehicles or stores.

* * *

At Sunnybank, Jane was in the drawing room, studying one of a pile of magazines that she had laid out on the floor. She looked up as he came in. 'Hello, dear, you're just in time to agree that these can be thrown away.'

De Silva looked over her shoulder at the gardening magazine. He didn't remember reading it, but then it was several years old. 'I suppose if you must,' he said. He raised an eyebrow and chuckled. 'What would you have done if I hadn't come in?'

'I'd have taken an executive decision.'

As they ate dinner, de Silva told her about the new development with Hank O'Halloran.

'I must admit, I'm surprised,' she said when he'd finished the story. 'But grief has a way of doing strange things to people. As long as Phoebe has plenty of protection, I hope her parents will allow her to accompany him. It sounds as if it will mean a lot to the poor man.'

De Silva hadn't been sure of how she would react to O'Halloran's plan. Jane was always so practical and down-to-earth, but he knew that beneath that lay an under-standing of the needs of others that prevented her from dismissing them outright, just because they didn't accord with her own opinions.

'Do you believe it's possible to talk the dead?' he asked. 'It must be one of the few subjects we've never discussed.'

'It's certainly not anything I've experienced, but I know that many people who lost loved ones and friends in the Great War turned to spiritualism when religion didn't pro-vide them with the consolation they sought. I remember how, back in England, people experimented with séances, table tapping, ouija boards, and all kinds of things in the hope of communicating beyond the grave.'

'And you think it was always taken seriously?'

'Most of the time, although I expect there were people who indulged in the pastime as a game and found a thrill in frightening themselves. Sir Arthur Conan Doyle famously became a firm believer towards the end of his life and refused to recant even when some people mocked him.'

'That seems strange. In the stories that you've given me to read, his detective, Sherlock Holmes, always reaches the solution to his cases by the most rational of means.'

'Yes, it does seem contradictory, but Conan Doyle spoke up in favour of spiritualism on many occasions, and after he died, a spiritualist meeting attended by thousands of people was held in his honour at the Royal Albert Hall in London. That's a very grand, beautiful building near a lovely park. Concerts are often held there. I went to several when I lived in London. At the meeting, the widow and Sir Arthur's family sat on the stage, but one chair was left empty for him. Many people claimed they felt his presence among them and even saw a shadow in the chair.'

De Silva nodded. It was interesting. Both his own religion and the Hindu religion of the Tamils acknowledged that there were spirits who existed in the same world as humans, but he had never thought about the views of other religions. 'It's amazing the things you know,' he said with a grin. 'How did you find all of this out?'

'Oh, quite easily. It's not all that many years since Sir Arthur died. Less than ten, I think, and I remember reading about it in the papers. In any case,' she continued briskly, 'I don't think it matters very much what I believe, Shanti. The important thing is that it may comfort Mr O'Halloran and Phoebe.'

'I went to have a look at the street where this woman lives. It's been a long time since I was in that part of town. It seems reasonably respectable, even if the house itself is dilapidated.'

'How did Marie hear of this woman in the first place?'

'Archie told me it was while they were in Calcutta.'

'If her name has spread that far, let's hope it's a good sign. It would be terribly sad if she's a charlatan. I suppose she wants money?'

'No doubt, but if O'Halloran's set on seeing her, as he appears to be, that's unlikely to put him off.'

'When will you go?'

'Tomorrow. I'm meeting Prasanna and Nadar at the police station. That reminds me, I must find out if we need to be in plain clothes. Patterson will come along with O'Halloran and Phoebe in one of the Residence's cars. Either Patterson's got the wind up now, or he's blameless. As far as Prasanna and Nadar have seen, he's been assiduous in attending to his duties since the kidnapping. Obviously, we need to ensure Patterson doesn't recognise them, so we'll have to be particularly careful.'

He scooped another spoonful of jackfruit curry onto his rice. 'But Archie's had no information from Scotland Yard yet, so I don't think there's any more we can do about Mr Patterson for the moment.'

CHAPTER 16

De Silva woke before dawn and was unable to get back to sleep. Thoughts of what lay ahead jumbled in his brain. At one moment, he convinced himself that it was a harmless excursion to comfort a bereaved father, at another, that it was unwise to take Phoebe away from the protection of the Residence. Had the kidnappers really only been interested in Marie? What if they had instructions to seize Phoebe Tankerton if the chance presented itself? And even more alarming, what if he was right about Patterson being behind the crime? He would have to watch the man with great care.

Eventually, he decided that sleep was not going to come. Slipping quietly out of bed, he pulled on trousers and tunic and went out into the garden. The grass was damp with dew, and the rising sun streaked the sky with pink and gold.

Down in the vegetable patch, the tiny runner beans he had noticed on his previous tour were swelling nicely. They would be good to eat soon. They were especially tasty when sizzled with curry leaves, onions, green chillies, and turmeric. He bent to lift a hank of the heavy foliage that had broken loose of its moorings and fix it back to its bean pole, then stopped. Something had been digging at the roots of the plant, leaving some of the lower leaves lying dead on the earth. It must be those wretched squirrels again. Maybe he would give Anif some powdered chilli to sprinkle on the area to discourage them, but then, he sighed, they would only move to another place.

Returning to the house, he heard the telephone ring. It seemed none of the servants were about to answer it, so he quickened his step.

'Ah good, you're up, de Silva.' It was Charlie Frobisher. 'The boss says you're to come in plain clothes.'

'Have my men been informed?'

'Don't worry. I dealt with that before they left here.'

In the bedroom, Jane was awake. 'Who was it on the telephone?' she asked.

'Only Frobisher telling me the three of us are to come in plain clothes. Archie was concerned that O'Halloran might be unhappy about an obvious police presence, and presumably, he was right.'

* * *

Meeting Prasanna and Nadar at the police station as arranged, de Silva took the precaution of concealing his Webley under his civilian jacket. They set off for Ridgeway Road and arrived shortly before the car from the Residence bringing O'Halloran, Phoebe, Frobisher, and Patterson was due. He wanted to be first, so that he had time to station Prasanna and Nadar discreetly, where they would be able to watch the building from outside. He told them to stay out of sight, not only in case danger lurked, but also so that Patterson wouldn't see them. Even though they weren't in police or Residence servants' uniform this time, it might be one encounter too many. But they were to be ready to move in if they saw anything untoward.

His preparations complete, he watched the car from the Residence drive slowly down the crowded street. Charlie Frobisher, who was driving, honked the horn at regular intervals to negotiate a path through the mass of shoppers, trucks, rickshaws, and carts to reach the place where the Morris was parked. De Silva got out and went over to greet them. He pointed to the house. 'I believe that's the place we want.'

Patterson nodded. 'You'd better go and knock.'

As he crossed the road, de Silva scowled. Even if Patterson didn't intend it, his tone of voice made everything he said sound like a command.

It was some time before a grouchy-looking servant answered the door. De Silva gave the medium's name and the man nodded. 'She is waiting for you, sahib.'

'Good.'

De Silva returned to the car to speak to O'Halloran. 'She's ready for you and Miss Tankerton, sir.'

Leaving Frobisher in charge of the car, de Silva, Patterson, Phoebe, and O'Halloran crossed the road, with Patterson taking the lead. Steep flights of stairs led to the top floor where the medium had her apartment. To their right, there were three doors ranged along the wall, but only two on the left. The servant went to the one at the front of the building, knocked and opened it. Patterson brushed past him and was about to enter when O'Halloran quickly stepped forward and put a hand on his shoulder.

'No need for that,' the American said firmly. 'You can wait out here.'

Reluctantly, Patterson gave way.

O'Halloran nodded. 'Thank you.'

He held out his hand to Phoebe who had been hanging back. 'Shall we go in?' All the colour had drained from her face. 'No need to be afraid,' he added gently.

Phoebe shook her head. 'I'm not. Marie would never want to hurt us.'

The little exchange gave de Silva the opportunity to peer into the room. He hadn't been sure what to expect – perhaps a scene out of the Arabian Nights with silken drapes and divans, or a magical-looking cave – but the place was surprisingly ordinary, and sparsely furnished. There were armchairs on either side of the windows, and in the centre of the room, four heavily carved, upright chairs encircled a round table covered with a velvet cloth in a drab shade of green. To his left, there was a bed, and a partly screened-off area fitted up as a rudimentary kitchen.

The only touch of drama came from the lack of light. The curtains had been drawn across the windows, and either there was no electricity, or the medium wanted to create a mystical atmosphere, for the room was illuminated by candles. A line of them guttered on the mantelpiece and two tall crimson ones burned in ornate brass candlesticks that stood on the table. A weighty, leather-bound book lay between them, but de Silva was too far away to see what was written on the open pages. The scent of tallow combined with stale air was unpleasant. He suspected the windows were rarely opened.

A woman swathed from head to toe in a purple robe glittering with gold and silver embroidery, emerged out of the shadows. A veil covered the lower half of her face. She wore black net gloves, the gloved fingers loaded with gaudy rings. Her dark eyes watched them shrewdly from under bushy black eyebrows. From what little de Silva was able to see, she was dark-skinned. She glanced at de Silva, Phoebe, and Patterson who were still outside the room.

'We must be alone if I am to summon your daughter's spirit,' she said to O'Halloran. She spoke in English, but with an accent de Silva couldn't place.

O'Halloran gestured to Phoebe. 'This young lady was close to her. I want her to stay.'

The medium peered at Phoebe. 'You came here before,' she said. 'You may stay if you wish.'

O'Halloran made a dismissive gesture in Patterson's and de Silva's direction. 'You heard the lady. Wait outside.'

Patterson scowled. 'I've got my orders not to let Miss Tankerton out of my sight unless I've checked out the place where I leave her.'

The irritable expression on O'Halloran's face intensified but eventually he nodded. 'If Madame Batavi agrees to it.' He looked at the medium who nodded. 'Then make it quick, Patterson,' he snapped.

De Silva followed Patterson into the room, his footsteps loud on the tiled floor. He recognised the blue and white patterns that he'd seen in some of the old Dutch buildings in Colombo. This house must be a hundred and fifty years old or more.

A black curtain on the wall to their right drew his attention. As another lodger's room must be beyond the wall, the curtain was in the wrong place for a window. He pointed to it. 'What's behind there?'

The medium didn't answer. Was it that she didn't understand, or did she not want to tell him? Patterson strode purposefully to the curtain and pulled it aside to reveal a large mirror.

The medium shrank back, her expression a mixture of anger and alarm.

'Mirrors must be covered when there's been a death.' She looked at O'Halloran. 'We must not anger the spirits if you wish to hear from your daughter.'

De Silva recalled how his grandmother had insisted on the mirrors in her house being kept covered after his grandfather's death. Like many people in Ceylon, she had believed that not to do so brought bad luck.

O'Halloran stepped forward and tugged the curtain across again. 'Are you done, Patterson?'

Patterson grunted an assent.

'Then off you go – you too, Inspector.'

In the corridor, with the door firmly closed behind them, de Silva noticed that the servant who had let them in had gone, presumably to return to his post downstairs. Patterson reached in his pocket and produced a pack of cigarettes; he held it out to de Silva. 'Do you smoke?'

Reluctant to refuse the civil offer, de Silva accepted one, even though he wasn't in the habit of smoking. They lit up, then Patterson walked down the landing, opening doors as he went. To the right of the stairs, the first two led into empty rooms about the size of the one the medium occupied, but then came a small bathroom, presumably for the use of all the occupants of the floor. The door on the opposite wall was locked.

'I wonder why.' De Silva frowned.

'It's probably unimportant,' said Patterson with a shrug. He sat down on the chair that stood against the opposite wall. He didn't appear to be in the mood for further conversation, so de Silva left him alone.

After ten minutes, Patterson finished a second cigarette and ground the butt under his heel. He glanced at his watch. 'How much longer do you think all this is going to take?'

'I've no idea, sir.'

'I thought you people knew all about this humbug.'

Determined not to let Patterson get under his skin, de Silva gave him a polite smile. 'In Ceylon, we have many different beliefs, as I understand you do in your country.'

Patterson gave another grunt and fell to staring at the floor as if he was trying to memorise every dent and scratch in the wood. In the silence, de Silva strained to make out what was being said in the medium's room, but the door was made of stout wood; all he heard was the murmur of voices, an occasional thud, and some creaking and rapping noises. He remembered Jane's remarks about table tapping and ouija boards. Presumably the noises were attributable to some such activity. He imagined that in a darkened room lit by wavering candlelight, people who had intended to treat the experience as a thrilling game might, in the heat of the moment, find they were experiencing more powerful emotions than they had bargained for. He hoped Phoebe Tankerton wasn't frightened. She had already been through enough.

Patterson got up and paced the landing. 'This is ridiculous,' he growled. 'The old girl's taking O'Halloran for a ride. I expect she'll ask for a wad of money when it's all over.'

He kicked a loose corner of the skirting board and, honeycombed with rot, the wood crumbled. De Silva wondered if the house had termites or some other wood-boring insect infestation to add to its attraction.

Patterson poked a finger into a crack in the wall and prised away a chunk of plaster. 'Damned place is ready to fall about our ears,' he muttered. He shot a sour look at de Silva. 'The sooner I get the Tankertons out of this godforsaken hole of a country and back to England, the better.'

De Silva didn't rise to the bait. It might be an act anyway. He was more concerned by the silence that appeared to have fallen in the room. A chill crept into his bones as he rapped on the door and then pressed his ear to it. No sound came from within. He tried again. Still no answer.

'Mr O'Halloran, sir! Is everything alright? Mr O'Halloran? Open the door, please.'

Again no answer. He tried to open the door. It was locked.

Patterson pushed past him and started to hammer on it, shouting out Phoebe's and O'Halloran's names. De Silva saw there were beads of sweat on his forehead. Finally, he took a step backwards then lunged at the door, ramming his shoulder against it. It barely shook. By now, Patterson's face had turned red. He rounded on de Silva 'What are you waiting for, man? Give me a hand.'

But after several attempts, the door still wouldn't budge.

'There's only one thing for it,' said Patterson, pulling out a gun from inside his jacket. 'Mr O'Halloran!' he shouted. 'Keep everyone away from the door!'

There was still no answer.

Patterson held the muzzle of the gun close to the lock and fired, then kicked the door open. De Silva took in the scene that met their eyes, and a feeling of numbness came over him.

CHAPTER 17

Sprawled on the floor with a chair half over him, as if he had upended it trying to pull himself to his feet, O'Halloran was alone in the room. His hands were tied behind his back, and a gag forced his mouth into a grotesque parody of a smile. The candles on the mantelpiece were still burning, but the two on the table were out. One of them had fallen out of its candlestick and lay on the open book. A pool of rapidly congealing wax spread like a bloodstain across the page. There was a pungent odour of singed paper and tallow. It was fortunate, thought de Silva, that a fire hadn't started; the building was probably dry as tinder. But what alarmed him more was what he saw on the right-hand wall.

The curtain that had covered the mirror had been pulled aside, as had the mirror itself, to reveal a hole in the wall about the size of a doorway. Patterson was already going through it. Briefly, de Silva deliberated whether he should follow him straight away or stop to help O'Halloran. He decided on the latter. Crouching down beside him, he removed the gag and undid the rope around his wrists.

'What happened, sir? Are you hurt?'

Feebly, O'Halloran shook his head then winced. 'Just dizzy. I was hit over the head, but I'll be okay. It's Phoebe you need to worry about. They came through that hole in the wall and took her away. Get after them.'

De Silva saw there was some blood in his hair, but he

decided to believe him when he claimed he wasn't badly injured. Hurrying through the door after Patterson, he found that the room he entered was empty apart from a pile of rubble and some tools, including a heavy hammer and a pickaxe. A few floorboards had been torn up, presumably to provide the wood that braced the rough opening in the wall. The other difference between the room and the one where he had left O'Halloran was the door to his left; it was open. He headed for it and went through.

What little light there was came from a skylight, but from the direction he was going in, his guess was that he was inside the archway that he had noticed spanning the houses on either side of the market lane. He emerged into the house on the other side and eventually found Patterson on the ground floor.

'They got away,' Patterson said angrily. 'There's a door back there.' He pointed to the rear of the hallway.

De Silva's heart sank. This was a disaster. 'Please go and find out if Mr Frobisher saw anything,' he said. 'I had better return to Mr O'Halloran. He needs help.'

Back in the medium's room, O'Halloran had dragged himself to a chair and sat with his head in his hands. He looked up at the sound of de Silva's footsteps and groaned. 'I can see from your face you were too late.' He swayed and would have fallen out of the chair if de Silva hadn't reached him quickly and steadied him.

'I'll find you some water, sir.'

In the kitchen area, he found a kettle with a few inches of water in the bottom, a china teapot with some tea left in it, and two small, bowl-shaped cups. One had a faint brown stain at the bottom; the other was clean. Quickly, de Silva put the palm of his hand against the kettle. The metal was warm. He would take the chance that it contained what was left of the water that had been boiled for the tea. He poured some into the clean cup and returned to O'Halloran, then waited until he had finished drinking.

'Can you tell me what happened?'

O'Halloran nodded, but he spoke very slowly, turning the empty cup round and round in his hands as he did so.

'The séance was underway. We'd been offered some tea.' His expression filled with pain. 'Phoebe didn't want it. I knew she'd say no. Marie used to kid her that she must be the only English person in the world who hated tea. In case Madame Batavi got offended by both of us refusing, I thought I'd better drink it.' He grimaced. 'That turned out to be a big mistake.'

'What do you mean?'

'I think she'd put something in it.'

The tea remaining in the pot had smelt perfectly normal to de Silva. If O'Halloran had been drugged, the medium must have added something to his cup.

'Then she had us staring into the flames of the candles on the table. Very soon I started to feel groggy. It was like I was in a crazy dream.'

He wiped his forehead.

'I saw Phoebe looking at me strangely. She got up and started towards me but then Madame Batavi also stood up and grabbed her from behind, covering her face with a cloth. Phoebe must have passed out, because she fell on the floor. I tried to go and help her, but my legs wouldn't do what I wanted. I saw Madame Batavi pick up one of the candlesticks. She smashed it on my head, and I went down. She'd gagged me before I had time to recover and shout for help and then tied my hands.' A tear rolled down his cheek. 'Some sucker, I've been,' he said hoarsely. 'Knocked out by a woman.'

'You said that "they" took Miss Tankerton away, sir. Did you see what the other people looked like?'

O'Halloran looked at him miserably. 'Not clearly, but I don't need to. It's the same guys who took Marie, isn't it, Inspector?'

'We don't know that for certain.'

He heard a sound and, going into the other room, found Frobisher.

'What's happening downstairs?' asked de Silva.

'We've been watching all the time. We saw no one leave the house apart from the servant who let you in. We thought he must be going out on an errand. I understand from Patterson the kidnappers got Phoebe out another way. He's insisted on heading off to search for her. I suppose a white girl would be very conspicuous in this area, but I'm not getting my hopes up.'

De Silva was alarmed at the prospect of his chief suspect being free to join someone who might be his latest victim.

'Don't worry, I found your men and they've gone with him,' Frobisher added quickly, clearly reading his mind. 'And I'm sure he's far too preoccupied to recognise them, so you needn't be alarmed on that score.'

Wretchedly, de Silva thought of the length of time he had waited before breaking into the room. It was probably much too late to find Phoebe.

O'Halloran was trying to stand up. He went to help him.

'If you're ready to walk, sir, we'd better get you back to the Residence. I'd like Doctor Hebden to take a look at you.'

* * *

As they slowly descended the stairs, thoughts raced through de Silva's mind. He wished he hadn't accepted Patterson's lack of concern about the door to the room next to the medium's being locked. Had it been deliberate on Patterson's part, to throw him off the scent? Once O'Halloran was safely away, he needed to search both buildings. Hopefully, there would be clues there that would tell them something about the kidnappers.

The servant who had let them into the house hadn't

116

returned from his supposed "errand"; maybe he was someone who had just been hired to pose as caretaker for a couple of hours. Outside, they got O'Halloran to the car. When he had closed the passenger door, Frobisher paused a moment. 'I hardly need tell you this is going to put the cat among the pigeons. Shall I try to keep it between ourselves and the boss for the moment?'

De Silva nodded and thanked him.

As Frobisher drove O'Halloran away, de Silva saw Patterson, Prasanna, and Nadar already coming back. Clearly, Patterson had given up the search.

With de Silva's agreement, Patterson took Prasanna with him to search the second house. Accompanied by Nadar, de Silva worked his way up from floor to floor in the first one, swiftly checking each room as they came to it. Apart from the one next to the séance room, none of them were locked and, in several of them, there was evidence that someone had been using them quite recently. In one, they found a moth-ridden mattress and a heap of stained bedding; in another, a tin can that smelt of axle grease showed traces of ash. A stick, charred at one end, and a smaller tin can lay beside it, grains of burnt rice were stuck to the bottom. From a corner of the room, a trail of mouse droppings led to a metal plate smeared with curry sauce. De Silva was sure he heard scuffling and squeaking behind the skirting boards. The smell of dry rot was everywhere, and the floors and what little furniture there was, were coated in a thick layer of dust. He noticed, however, that in a few places, the dust was absent or scuffed, as if furniture and ornaments had been removed quite recently. Had the servant been living there as a caretaker, or was there someone else?

By the time they reached the top landing, Prasanna and Patterson were back in the medium's room. Patterson was looking grim.

'Well?' he barked, swinging around to glare at de Silva.

'Someone's been in the building and not long ago, but they're not here now.'

'What in the hell were you doing letting O'Halloran get away with this mad idea of his?' exploded Patterson. 'It should never have been allowed to happen in the first place.'

Refraining from saying that as far as he knew, Patterson hadn't argued vociferously against it at the time, de Silva listened to the man's rant, but finally, his patience ran out.

'I can't answer your questions, but if we are to work together—' He paused to allow a moment where a "sir" might have dropped in but did not. 'I suggest we do so in a spirit of co-operation and attempt to remain calm.'

Patterson glowered and mumbled something but fell silent.

It was the closest thing he was likely to get to an apology, thought de Silva; he didn't press the point. Loath as he was to give Patterson the benefit of the doubt, if he was innocent, the Englishman probably wasn't relishing the prospect of telling his employers the news. On the other hand, if the suspicion of him was justified, he would be reaching the crucial stage in his plan where he needed to convince everyone that he was furious at being caught out by the kidnappers. In that case, he needed to react strongly, however objectionable that made him.

CHAPTER 18

On arrival at the Residence, de Silva found that Hank O'Halloran had been taken to his room to rest. Doctor Hebden and Archie were with him. It would be a good idea to find out how much they already knew and also, to be sure that O'Halloran's condition was no worse, so de Silva asked to be taken to them.

When he was shown in, Hebden was shining a small torch into O'Halloran's right eye. 'Just a precaution,' he said. 'Try and follow the light, Mr O'Halloran.'

O'Halloran blinked at the brightness but did as he was asked.

Hebden clicked off the torch and nodded to de Silva. 'I don't think there's anything to worry about, just running the usual tests. You should be right as rain in a day or two, Mr O'Halloran, but I'll come and see you again tomorrow. Send for me sooner if you have any dizziness or vomiting. I suppose the old head's still throbbing a bit?'

'You could say that.'

'Get some sleep if you can. I'll arrange for painkillers to be sent over from the surgery.'

De Silva and Archie followed Hebden from the room. 'I don't think it's anything serious,' he said when they were out of earshot. 'Head injuries are always a concern, but he looks to have been lucky. Have the Tankertons been told what's happened yet?'

'They're about to be,' said Archie. 'When I heard the news, they were still out on an afternoon drive to the Botanic Gardens. My wife was hoping that getting them out of the house might take their minds off things. Frobisher tells me they're back now.'

'I'll wait here until they've been told. It may be advisable to prescribe a sedative for Mrs Tankerton.'

* * *

In Archie's study, Patterson was silent for once, a morose expression on his face as de Silva filled in the details of the disaster for Archie's benefit. It provided no relief that his boss looked more appalled than angry.

'This passage you found must have come as a nasty surprise,' said Archie frowning. 'Dashed inconvenient it was there for them to get away by, but I believe it wasn't uncommon in the early days for merchants to use one house for their business premises and an adjoining one for their residence.'

He sighed. 'What's done is done. Let's pray the outcome won't be as disastrous as it was last time.' He hauled himself out of his chair. 'Time to face the music, gentlemen. The girl's parents have to be informed.'

* * *

Driving back to Sunnybank, de Silva felt as if a stone had settled in his gut. He wouldn't forget the expressions on the Tankertons' faces for a long time. Two people desperate for news they dreaded to hear.

Archie had done his best to be reassuring, as had Florence. Even Florence's little household mop of a dog, Angel, had seemed subdued by this new tragedy, but de

Silva was certain nothing had given the Tankertons comfort. It was probably for the best that O'Halloran had not made an appearance.

He slowed at the entrance to the drive and turned in. Jane was in the drawing room writing a letter.

'Shanti dear! You look as if you've seen a ghost. Whatever's happened now?'

'You might do better to ask what hasn't happened, my love,' he said grimly.

He explained what had gone on that morning. 'It's extraordinary,' she said when he'd finished. 'That these people should be so bold as to strike twice. Poor Grace and Walter Tankerton. My heart goes out to them. And Hank O'Halloran too. First his own grief, now this. What are you all going to do now?'

'Wait, I suppose. What else can we do? I'm sure there'll be a ransom note. The question is, if the Tankertons pay, as they insist that they will, can we be sure that the kidnappers will honour their side of the bargain?'

Jane shivered. 'This man Patterson had no business being rude. I don't like the sound of him at all, even if he is innocent.'

De Silva shrugged. 'If he is, I wouldn't blame him for being worried about being sacked by the Tankertons. It wouldn't have helped matters to lose my temper.'

'Well, I think you're being far too generous, and I sincerely hope he does get the sack.'

De Silva smiled. 'Thank you for that ferocious defence, my love, but getting Phoebe Tankerton safely home is the most important thing.'

Jane sighed. 'Of course it is.'

'And although Patterson was in my sight from the moment we went into the house until the kidnap, we shouldn't lose sight of the possibility that he's involved.'

Jane looked pensive for a moment. 'Apart from O'Halloran, her parents, Residence staff, and you, Prasanna and Nadar, was he the only other person who knew about the appointment with the medium, and that Phoebe was going too?'

'Yes. And that's a good point. I suspect that if he is guilty, he's more likely to give himself away if he believes it's easy to push me around. For the same reason, we must discourage the Tankertons from dispensing with his services at the moment. If he's free to leave Nuala, we would have to arrest him, then boom go our chances of catching him out.'

'Bang, dear.'

A more sinister thought also crossed de Silva's mind. It was that if Patterson was arrested, leaving his accomplices in sole charge of Phoebe, what might they do? Without instructions and, worse still from their point of view, money, they might simply kill her and vanish. Regardless of other considerations, it was definitely best to delay arresting Patterson until Phoebe was safe.

He picked up a rose petal that had fallen from the arrangement in the crystal vase on the table beside his chair. Absentmindedly, he rolled it between his thumb and forefinger, crushing the delicate tissue and releasing its fragrance. 'If only we'd searched more thoroughly before we left Phoebe in that room,' he said, half to himself.

'You're not to blame. You weren't to know Madame Batavi had anything to do with the kidnapping gang. Certainly, most people wouldn't have been suspicious about her not wanting you to uncover that mirror. In Victorian days, people used to cover mirrors when there'd been a death in the house. It's an old superstition that if you didn't, the spirit of the deceased would be caught in the glass.'

De Silva smiled. 'Yes. One not forgotten in Ceylon. Many people still hold beliefs about the dangers of mirrors. I was completely taken in.'

'Don't be too hard on yourself, dear. O'Halloran was too and, if he's innocent, so was Patterson.'

'I'd like to find out more about the houses in Ridgeway Road. I'll go over again later and see if any other residents have turned up. I left Prasanna and Nadar on watch. I'm afraid they may have another night or two away from home.'

'What are the houses like?'

'From the architecture, old – my guess is from the time of the Dutch, and in extremely poor condition. By the look of them, whoever lives there isn't too particular. I want to know who owns them, and if Madame Batavi was the only occupier, why. Most people with property of that size don't leave it empty. They want to make money. The only conclusion I can reach is that the aim was to be there unobserved. So, we are hunting for someone who had enough money to take both houses, or who owned them in the first place. That is where your British love of keeping records of everything will be useful. Tomorrow, I'll go to the Town Hall and ask to see the census for Ridgeway Road.'

CHAPTER 19

A day passed, and no one came back to Ridgeway Road, nor could anything be done about a wider search. Walter and Grace Tankerton flatly refused to countenance one. They were convinced that the kidnappers had got wind of the planned search in Marie O'Halloran's case and that had precipitated her murder.

'The boss telephoned William Petrie in Kandy,' said Charlie Frobisher, calling de Silva at home as he was about to have breakfast. 'Petrie's ruled that on no account are we to go against the Tankertons' wishes.'

'What about Patterson?'

'Very subdued. We're making sure he's watched by Residence staff, but I'm not sure what to make of him. So far, the Tankertons have said nothing about his future, and it's hard to know what they're thinking. But Walter must be a clever man to have made all his money. I'd be surprised if it hasn't occurred to him that not many people knew that his daughter was accompanying O'Halloran on the trip to the medium.'

'Are you suggesting he might think that the obvious one who's not above suspicion is Andrew Patterson?'

'Something like that.'

'The same thought occurred to my wife and me. I wonder if Tankerton will say anything.'

'Interesting to see if he does. My guess is that in that

event, the boss's advice will be to wait until we have Phoebe back before taking action.'

'And I've little doubt that Tankerton would agree with him.'

After he'd breakfasted, de Silva set off for the Town Hall. Despite the embargo on a search, he considered it was a safe enough thing to do.

The high-ceilinged, marble-floored hall echoed to the sound of people coming and going, and a battery of fans whirred overhead, stirring the tepid air. At a reception counter of highly polished, treacle-brown wood, a row of officials was helping with enquiries. He went up to one of them, showed his warrant card and asked to see the census records for Ridgeway Road. Told to wait, an hour passed before he was shown to a small room where a pile of cardboard files had been put on a table for him. Searching them for entries in Ridgeway Road didn't turn out to be easy; the writing was often cramped and barely legible, as if the writer had been commanded to save paper at all costs. On more than one occasion, in order to decipher the words, he had to resort to the magnifying glass that, at Jane's suggestion, he had brought with him. The steady tick of the clock on the wall reminded him that hours were going by and he still had a lot to do.

After a break to go out to the bazaar to buy himself lunch, he eventually found a file that mentioned the two houses and showed them as being empty. He put it aside and started on the next one back in the same bundle, but that gave no name for an occupier either. By the time he had finished studying them all, he had still found no record of anyone living in the buildings.

He returned to the entrance desk and asked if there were any other files he might see.

'There are older ones, but they are kept in the basement. If you wish to see them, you must make a requisition.'

'How long will that take?'

The official looked up to the ceiling as if the answer would be found there. 'A week,' he said at last. 'Maybe more.'

'That's far too long. I need the information today. Tomorrow at the latest.'

The man spread his hands. 'I am sorry.'

'The assistant government agent will be concerned to hear of this lack of cooperation. It's of great importance that I see the files without delay.'

A resigned expression came over the official's face. He pushed a form across the counter. 'Fill that in. I will see what can be done. Come back tomorrow.'

* * *

He hadn't been back at the station long when there was another telephone call from Charlie Frobisher.

'Ah, got hold of you at last, de Silva,' he said. 'A ransom note arrived at the Residence after we spoke this morning. Posted in Nuala like the first one. The Tankertons insist they'll pay it. As in O'Halloran's case, they've only been given until the day after tomorrow to find the money.'

'Who will hand it over?'

'I'm not sure. That needs to be discussed. The letter says there'll be another one on the day of the handover stipulating the place.'

This differed from the instructions for the handover in Marie O'Halloran's kidnap. De Silva was trying to think whether that was significant when a commotion in the outer office distracted him. As he was on his own, he said goodbye to Frobisher and went out to investigate. So long as Patterson remained at the Residence, his whereabouts could be monitored, so he had left Prasanna and Nadar on duty at Ridgeway Road. It would be a pity if this was something that it would be good experience for them to deal with.

The noise in the outer office was caused by an indignant stallholder from the bazaar, complaining about the behaviour of the fruit seller on the stall next to his.

'Every day, this man throws his unsold fruit under my stall rather than take it away. He knows I store my goods underneath. No one will buy my first-rate leather bags – all of them top brands – when they are stained with bad juice from rotten mangoes and other fruits.'

De Silva doubted if any bags in Nuala's bazaar were from the top brands, but he agreed to come along with the stallholder and speak to his neighbour. This resulted in an event that took up a considerable amount of what was left of the afternoon and involved, as far as de Silva could see, pretty well every relative and close friend that the two men possessed.

Having reached an outcome that appeared to satisfy both parties, he was about to return to the station when a nearby disturbance attracted his attention. When he went to find out what was the matter, he found a local woman sobbing and wringing her hands. Her olive-green sari was torn. At first, he was afraid that she had been attacked.

'What's happened here?' he asked one woman in the crowd that had gathered, but in the hubbub, she seemed not to hear him. Some of the others were reaching out and trying to console the weeping woman, although she was too agitated to take any notice.

De Silva's eye fell on an elderly man who stood a little apart from the rest, leaning on a stick. He repeated his question. The elderly man shifted his weight and, raising the stick, pointed the tip of it at a nearby doorway. 'That is where she lives. She came home from her work and found her husband's body. She says he has been murdered.'

* * *

Not all of the crowd around the woman failed to react to the sight of de Silva's uniform. Some abandoned their efforts to comfort the widow and followed him into the house.

Inside, the dead man's body lay face down across the threshold between the living room and the kitchen. The blade of a chopping knife had been driven deep into his back. A woman peering over de Silva's shoulder shrieked and fainted. 'Take her out of here,' he said testily. 'Find some water for her to drink when she comes to.'

The woman was carried away, and an expectant hush fell over the remaining observers as de Silva knelt down beside the body. It was stiff and cold. The man must have been murdered at some time in the night.

'Is he dead, sahib?' one of the men asked.

De Silva nodded. 'I want everyone out of here and the door of the house locked until the body can be removed.' He sighed inwardly. 'Then you had all better tell me what you saw, but one at a time.'

* * *

Several hours later, he decided that he had learnt all he was likely to from the murdered man's neighbours, and none of it was going to be of much help. Mainly, he discovered that the man, whose name was Romesh, had been unpopular. His wife was a cleaner at the Crown Hotel, but no one knew what job he did. She usually only worked a night shift and came home in the day, but for once, she had gone to see a sick friend when she finished her work.

'I see him hanging around his house all the time,' said an old woman with betel-stained teeth. A gobbet of spit fell from her mouth onto the ground. 'There is never enough money in the house. Poor Achala cooks and cleans and works her fingers to the bone for him, the lazy dog.'

'Did you see him go out sometimes?'

'He usually went out after dark,' one man piped up. There was a general murmur of agreement.

'To drink and play cards,' the old woman added disparagingly.

'Where did he get the money from?'

Her expression turned even more sour. 'Stole it from Achala, I expect.'

If all this was true, de Silva began to wonder why Romesh's widow was so distressed at losing her husband. There was no accounting for love.

Questioning over, he ascertained that the couple had no children, but there were family members who would temporarily take the widow in and look after her. Leaving her in their hands, he went back into the house, locking the door behind him to keep out curious neighbours. For now, he should at least cover Romesh's body, and he wanted to take the knife to the police station and check it for finger-prints. If he found any, he would try to find a way of taking Patterson's to see if they were a match.

After he had done those jobs, he took a final look around. On a shelf, there was a gaudily framed photograph showing Achala and Romesh together in younger days. Both were in what looked to be their best clothes, and they were garlanded with flowers and smiling happily. Perhaps it had been their wedding day. The marriage might at least have begun well. Briefly, he wondered whether to take the photograph for a few days. The widow wasn't likely to come back to the house for some time, so she needn't know, and it might be useful. He decided he would.

On his return to the station, he checked the knife for fingerprints but there were none. Either the killer had wiped the handle clean, or they had worn gloves. A telephone call to the operator established there had been no calls from Kandy or anywhere else since he went out. He also telephoned the Residence and spoke to Charlie Frobisher as Archie was not available.

'I'm afraid I'm the bringer of more bad news.'

'I'm sorry to hear that,' said Frobisher.

'There's been a murder at the bazaar.' De Silva outlined the afternoon's events.

'Leave it with me, and I'll tell the boss when he comes back. Do you think there's a connection to our cases?'

'Too early to say, but I think we can't rule it out. I understand that the deceased's widow works as a cleaner at the Crown Hotel. I may be able to get some information about the family there.' De Silva thought of his friend, Sanjeewa, the deputy manager.

'No more news to report from this end. Oh, and don't worry about your chaps at Ridgeway Road. I'll see what can be done about relieving them soon.'

De Silva thanked him and made a mental note to stop at Prasanna's house on his way home to Sunnybank to warn Kuveni that she might have to wait to see her husband for a day or two. He would ask her to let Nadar's wife know.

Achala's husband's body would have to be dealt with in the morning. He hoped it was safe in the locked house; he had seen to it that it was decently covered before he left. He would speak to the undertakers and make the arrangements to fetch it as soon as possible. Under normal circumstances, it was left to Hindu families to make their own plans for funerals and the subsequent cremation that was customary in their religion, but these were not normal circumstances.

He must remember to talk to Archie too and find out if there was any financial help that could be offered to the widow, although it sounded as if her husband had been more of a drain on the family's finances than an asset to them.

* * *

An hour after dark, he arrived at home to find Jane in the drawing room, a puzzled expression on her face.

'Something wrong?'

'I'm sure I had some red wool in my sewing basket,' she said. 'But I can't find it.'

'Perhaps you finished it up and forgot,' said de Silva with a shrug.

Jane closed the wicker basket's lid. 'Ah well, I'll have to go down to Hatton for some more. I'm sure you're far too busy to drive me, but Emerald might like a trip.'

De Silva sat down heavily in his armchair; the seat cushion exhaled a little whump of air.

'Another bad day?' asked Jane sympathetically.

'I'm afraid so. I didn't have much luck at the Town Hall. I'll have to go back tomorrow, but I fear it may be a waste of time. The ransom note has arrived at the Residence, and now there's been a murder at the bazaar.'

'How dreadful,' she said when he came to the end of the story. 'Let's hope Archie agrees to give some money to the widow to help her out. She'll have the expenses of her husband's funeral to pay, and I doubt a cleaner at the Crown earns a great deal of money.'

'I'll go up there tomorrow. I hope Sanjeewa will be prepared to help her too. At the very least, she'll need time to grieve.'

'Have you thought about whether there's a connection to Marie O'Halloran's murder and the kidnap?'

'Yes, and Charlie Frobisher mentioned that too. I've nothing definite to go on,' he explained about the lack of fingerprints, 'but it's certainly unusual to have so many serious crimes close together in a small place like Nuala. Maybe my trip to the Crown will provide some enlightenment.'

He leant back in his armchair and yawned. 'I forgot to ask if you enjoyed that film you and Emerald went to see.'

'Under the circumstances, I'll forgive you,' said Jane with a smile. 'It was a comedy called *The Villiers Diamond*. Emerald and I both thought it was very entertaining.'

'Good.'

After dinner, they listened to some music until it was time for bed. Not Rachmaninoff this time, but Debussy, which was far more soothing. But even with Debussy's graceful, silvery music filling the room, de Silva found it impossible to relax. Two murders and two kidnappings in Nuala within the space of a few days. Surely, there was a connection, but what was it? What would Patterson have to do with the reprobate husband of poor Achala? Was there a clue in the drinking and gambling? Perhaps the old crone with the betel-stained teeth was wrong. Rather than stealing the money from his wife, he might have earned it, but in a most shameful way.

CHAPTER 20

As it so often did, sleep ironed out the tangle of thoughts in his head. If Romesh had been involved in the kidnap and been one of the men present when Marie O'Halloran was supposed to be handed over, Hank O'Halloran might recognise him. If he didn't, it wouldn't prove conclusively that Romesh had nothing to do with the crime, but if he did, it might be the lead they had been waiting for.

Before contacting the Residence to ask to speak to O'Halloran, de Silva telephoned the undertakers who promised to collect Romesh's body as soon as he had dropped off the key to the house with them. He looked at his watch. There was time to take the key, and visit the Crown, before he needed to collect O'Halloran.

* * *

'What can I do for you today, my friend?' asked Sanjeewa smiling, as de Silva was shown into his office. As he explained about the murder at the bazaar and the plight of the widow, Sanjeewa scratched his forehead.

'Achala the wife of Romesh... I don't recall the name, but we have many cleaners here. I'll speak to housekeeping. Maybe it's best not to mention murder, do you agree? The manager will not like gossip about one of the employee's family problems.'

'Understood.'

Sanjeewa reached for the internal telephone at his elbow and picked up the receiver. 'Get me housekeeping,' he said when someone answered. He tapped his fingers on the desktop as he waited.

'Hello, Mr Gunesekera here. One of the cleaners will not be in.' He gave Achala's name. 'She may stay off work with pay until I say otherwise.' He paused to listen then went on. 'There has been a sudden death in the family. Her husband.'

He listened again. 'Yes… good… I will speak with you about the new tablecloths later. Excellent, goodbye.' He put down the receiver. 'There, all is arranged. Does this Achala have family who will help her?'

'I believe so.'

'If she is in difficulties, let me know, and I'll see if something can be done for her.'

'That's good of you. In the meantime, if the staff who work with her can tell me anything about her circumstances, particularly her husband, it would be helpful.'

'I'll see what I can do.'

'Is there any chance of making enquiries speedily?'

Sanjeewa nodded. 'Important, eh? Leave it with me. Why don't you make yourself comfortable in one of our private rooms while you wait? I'll order you some tea.'

Half an hour, and several cups of tea later, Sanjeewa came to find him.

'I asked around a few people. A cleaner that this woman, Achala, often works with has become friendly with her. She says Achala is always complaining about her husband; particularly because he keeps company with a man that she does not like at all.'

'Why is that?'

'Achala says he is a very bad influence. Without him, her husband would never have taken to gambling and drinking as he did.'

136

'Did she know the man's name?'

'Not his full one. She said that Achala called him Johannes.'

'A European?'

'No, a local, but of course there must be Dutch stock in his ancestry.'

A few names going back to the time of the Dutch were still used in Ceylon, although fewer than those that, like his own, recalled the days of the Portuguese.

'Was she able to describe him to you?'

'No, she's never met him.'

But with luck, Achala would be able to. He would tackle her on the subject when she'd had a little more time to recover.

'Thank you, my friend. That is useful information. I'll bear it in mind.'

'Maybe Romesh fell out with this man. Perhaps, over money. I have it! Romesh was entrusted with some money to place a bet. He pretended to lose, but he had won and was trying to keep the money for himself. His friend found out and –'

De Silva laughed. 'Is this the plot for the first movie in your forthcoming film career? Without wishing to discourage you, it will have to be more compelling than that.'

'It is only in the early stages of development,' said Sanjeewa in a tone of mock indignation.

'Very well.'

'Filmmaking might be a more congenial way of earning my living than here,' he added gloomily. 'Keeping everyone on their toes is hard work, and now the new tablecloths for the dining room have arrived in the wrong sizes. Monkeys broke into one of the laundry rooms and everything must be washed and ironed again before it can be used. Our British manager is saying that we must cut our costs. I tell him you can't run a luxury hotel without breaking eggs.'

'I'm sorry to hear about your tribulations. I'll leave you to get on with them.'

'Oh, before you go, there's one more thing. I'm sorry, I should have told you earlier, but you are hard to find, my friend.'

'Yes?'

'An American came to reception asking for Mr O'Halloran. I happened to be in the vicinity and overheard, so I went to see if I could find out anything for you.'

'Did he give his name?'

Sanjeewa shook his head. 'I asked, but he ignored the question.'

'A pity. It might be useful to know.'

'I told him Mr O'Halloran had checked out, and we aren't sure if he's coming back.'

'Did he leave a message or say where he could be contacted?'

Again, Sanjeewa shook his head.

'What did he look like?'

'Well dressed in a dark suit and hat, although such clothes seem unsuitable for this climate. He was tall, with grey hair, glasses, and a small moustache.'

'If by a stroke of luck he returns, I'd like whoever speaks with him to get in touch with me straight away. If he can somehow be persuaded not to leave the hotel, say on the pretext that O'Halloran is visiting and you're looking for him, I'll come over.'

'I'll see what we can do.'

* * *

Later, after telling the undertakers they would be coming, de Silva drove over to the Residence to collect O'Halloran. The American was quiet on the way there.

'I appreciate your doing this for us, sir,' said de Silva when another of several silences fell. 'If you start to feel unwell however, please tell me, and I will take you back to the Residence straight away.'

O'Halloran gave a wry smile. 'I'm glad to help and you needn't be concerned about me. I'm getting tired of being told to rest. The only other time I've been out of the house is when my secretary came to visit me, and that dragon lady, Florence Clutterbuck, let her take me for a walk around the garden.'

The undertakers' premises were in the part of town where most of the British shops and offices were situated. Its frontage was taken up by a plate-glass window displaying a coffin with brass fittings. Wreathes of dusty-looking imitation flowers smothered the lid, and black drapes hung in the background. At the melancholy sight, a frisson of unease made de Silva shiver.

The manager greeted them, showing them into the parlour to wait for a few moments while the body was prepared for them to view it. The room reminded de Silva of the one at the vicarage where Reverend Peters received callers. It had the same sepulchral hush, as if no one ever raised a voice in there. A Turkish rug in muted colours covered the floor and the furniture was dark and unattractive. O'Halloran remained standing, so de Silva felt he should stand as well. In any case, the two overstuffed sofas, upholstered in buttoned red plush, looked uninviting.

Five minutes passed before they were ushered to the room where the body was laid out on a table. Even though numerous fans whirred on the ceiling in an attempt to keep the air cool, there was already an unpleasant smell fighting to defeat the pungent efforts of formaldehyde. Washed and shaved, Romesh's face had a strange, dummy-like appearance. As they came closer, de Silva noticed that the waxy pallor of his skin was tinged with grey.

O'Halloran was silent, studying Romesh's face. At last, he turned to de Silva. 'I'm sorry, Inspector. I've never seen this guy before.' He shook his head sadly. 'What about his family? I'd like to give something to help them out. Can you arrange for it to be handed over for me?'

De Silva was surprised at the generosity, but he nodded. 'Of course, sir. It's very kind of you.'

'You said on the way over here that his widow was a cleaner at the Crown, and that seemed to be their only means of support. If I were in her shoes, I hope someone would do the same for me.'

The sound of someone clearing their throat reminded de Silva that the manager of the undertakers was still in the room. He nodded to him. 'Thank you, we've seen enough.'

The man showed them out, and de Silva thanked him again and confirmed that Romesh's body could be released to his family. He and O'Halloran walked back to the Morris. The return journey passed mainly in silence. The Morris turned into the Residence's drive, and they were soon saying their goodbyes. Leaning in through the driver's window, O'Halloran put a hand on de Silva's shoulder and squeezed it with a firm grip. 'I'm sorry again that I was no help. You're doing a great job. Keep it up.'

CHAPTER 21

In the afternoon, de Silva returned to the Town Hall to speak to the clerk he had seen the previous day. 'I'm sorry, Inspector,' he said. 'The records are missing.'

De Silva frowned.

'But I spoke with one of my colleagues who has been here for many years,' the clerk went on. 'He may be able to tell you something about the place.'

De Silva thanked him and went to wait in the small room where he had looked at the files.

The elderly man who entered a few minutes later was stooped with age and dressed in a dark suit that hung loosely on his sparse frame. Through a gold pince-nez, he peered at de Silva with the air of a benign goat.

'I understand that you wanted to know about the two empty buildings in Ridgeway Road, Inspector. I'm able to help you there.' He adjusted his pince-nez with a liver-spotted hand.

'I'm much obliged to you.'

'They were built in the late seventeen-hundreds, when the Dutch were in Ceylon. In my early years here, forty years ago, the family that owned them was called de Groote. The de Grootes were descended from the original Dutch settlers and were well known and prosperous – one of the major exporters of sapphires from this island to Europe. However, there were difficulties and they fell on hard times.

One of the properties was turned into a lodging house, but it didn't sufficiently repair the family fortunes. The last of the male de Grootes to live in Nuala died in suspicious circumstances. The houses were locked up and his widow returned to Holland. I remember it because, at the time, it was the talk of the town.'

'Have any of the family been seen since?'

The elderly official shook his head. 'No. As you will have observed if you've been there, the houses are slowly decaying. From time to time, attempts have been made to trace any relatives who might do repairs on them, but without success.'

'Do you have any idea when the buildings were last occupied?'

'As far as I recall, no one has lived there since the last of the de Grootes left.' He peered more closely at de Silva. 'I'd like to think that my information is useful to you, Inspector but unfortunately, I see it's not.'

'I'm afraid you're right, sir, but thank you for your time.'

De Silva was getting up to leave when the elderly official raised a hand to stop him. 'There is something that might interest you, Inspector. A lady came here recently asking about empty houses in various districts.' He scratched his chin. 'I can find out easily enough for you if one of them was Ridgeway Road. Her visit was remarked on because the enquiry was an unusual one. She said she was trying to trace lost relatives, but not many ladies come here alone.'

'Can you tell me anything more about her?'

'I didn't see her myself, but if you'll wait, I'll see what I can find out for you.'

Settling down again, de Silva waited. Luckily, it wasn't long before he heard shuffling footsteps in the corridor, and the elderly official came in again.

'My colleagues tell me the lady was British. She was well dressed and looked to be in early middle age. She took a note of empty properties in several roads, including Ridgeway.'

'You say she came recently. Can you be more precise?'

'Yes, it was about two weeks ago.'

'Thank you, sir. That's most helpful.'

The elderly official smiled, showing wonky, yellowing teeth. 'I'm glad to have been of assistance. I don't wish to pry, but may I ask what your interest in this lady is?'

'A crime has been committed at a house in Ridgeway Road. Anyone expressing an interest in the houses there may be connected.'

'I see. Well, Inspector, if anyone else comes enquiring, I'll be sure to let you know.'

'Thank you again, sir.'

* * *

Driving away from the Town Hall, de Silva pondered this new information. Whoever had been living in the house was probably a squatter, but that didn't mean to say that there was no point trying to find out who they were. The lady claiming to be looking for her lost relatives might have some bearing on the case too. Unfortunately, to establish that, he would need to find her, and the description didn't give him a lot to go on. Perhaps he would concentrate on discovering the identity of the squatter first. He turned the Morris towards Ridgeway Road. He would take a stroll around. There was usually someone who liked to chew the fat and show off their mastery of local gossip.

* * *

At the fruit and vegetable market, he bought a small bunch of bananas and peeled and ate them one by one as he walked. They would have to do as a late lunch. Pausing to talk to any stallholders who weren't busy with customers, he engaged them in conversation for a few moments before bringing the topic round to the buildings he was interested in, and the lady searching for her relatives, but he didn't have any luck with finding out useful information. At a stall where he stopped to buy a bowl of coconut milk, however, his luck turned.

'That's Johannes you want to know about,' the stallholder said with a grin. 'Johannes!' he shouted to his neighbour. The neighbour let out a guffaw of laughter.

De Silva's ears pricked up. It was an unusual name, and the same one that the murdered man Romesh's friend bore. 'What can you tell me about him?' he asked.

'He'd have you believe he's descended from some rich Dutchmen from a long time ago, but I'd lay money on it he's no better than the rest of us.'

'Have you seen him around here recently?'

The stallholder thought for a moment. 'Not for a while, but that's nothing. He often wanders off for weeks at a time, then comes back with boastful tales of the places he's been.' He chuckled. 'As far as anyone knows, he's never even been as far as Hatton, so only the gods know where he hides himself away.'

This Johannes sounded an unusual character.

'Does he work at anything? What does he live on?'

The stallholder shrugged. 'He does a bit of sweeping up and odd jobs when they're needed at the cinema. He likes to talk about the films he sees when he's allowed to stand in at the back. He'll ramble on for hours if you let him.'

'Have you ever heard of him causing any trouble?'

'Trouble?' The stallholder shook his head. 'No.'

'Does he have family or friends?'

'No family I know of. Unless you count these mysterious grand relations that he likes to talk about. As for friends—'

He scratched his chin. 'Let me see. I've seen him around with one fellow, but I don't know his name.'

Although several serious crimes in the space of a few days didn't mean they were all connected, their happening in a small place like Nuala shortened the odds, so de Silva took the photograph of Romesh out of the pocket of his uniform jacket. He had temporarily removed it from its gaudy frame. 'Might it be this man?'

The stallholder studied the photograph then shrugged. 'It might be, but I'm not sure. Why do you ask?'

'He's had an accident,' said de Silva, quickly making up a story in his head in case the man asked more questions. 'We're trying to identify him, and we've reason to believe he may have a connection with the house where you say this Johannes lives. Maybe Johannes can help us.'

An elderly woman attended by two servants carrying her baskets paused by the stall; to his relief, de Silva saw the stallholder immediately lose interest in Romesh's fate. With a nod of thanks, he moved on. That had been a lucky break. All he needed now was for Johannes to return to the house and it might be possible to find out more about what Romesh had been doing to get himself killed.

* * *

'Johannes is certainly a Dutch name,' said Jane. 'If this man really is a descendant of a wealthy family, how sad for him to be reduced to living in such difficult circumstances.'

'We don't know he would be any better off in Holland. The de Grootes may never have repaired their fortune. Anyway, at least this Johannes has a roof over his head which is more than many do. And as he may be connected to the crimes, I wouldn't feel too sorry for him just yet.'

Jane sighed. 'I suppose so. Are Prasanna and Nadar still at the house?'

'Yes. I'll pay them another visit when I've finished my cup of tea. I'm hoping that Johannes won't be absent for much longer. I fear all the commotion at the house may have alarmed him. I must tell Prasanna and Nadar to be as unobtrusive as possible. I suspect he'll only come back if he thinks no one's there.'

He reached for a slice of butter cake and put it on his plate. 'Before you say anything, I had no lunch except for a few bananas.'

Jane smiled. 'I wasn't going to. About this Johannes again. From what we know of Romesh, and what that stallholder said, do you think it's more likely Romesh led Johannes astray rather than the other way around?'

'It seems quite likely.'

He bit off a corner of his piece of cake and munched it thoughtfully. 'I wonder how the two of them met. I think I'll go over to the cinema and speak to the manager. Apparently, Johannes does odd jobs there. And I have another piece of interesting information from Sanjeewa Gunesekera.'

He explained about the man asking for O'Halloran at the Crown.

'I wonder how he fits in,' said Jane. 'How do you think he knew Hank O'Halloran was in Nuala?'

'A lucky shot in the dark perhaps, but it's a great pity that we don't have more information. On the face of it, this man seems unlikely to have any connection to the cases we have in hand, but it's too soon to write anything off.'

He popped the last of his cake in his mouth and dusted the crumbs from his jacket.

'Delicious.'

'I'll tell cook,' Jane said with a smile. 'Will you be back for dinner?'

'I hope so, although if I go to see Prasanna and Nadar as well, I may be later than usual.'

* * *

The afternoon showing of a film had just finished. Going into the foyer, de Silva passed cinema goers coming out, chatting and laughing. The booth where tickets would be sold for the evening performance was shuttered, but a man was restocking the shelves behind the cigarette and sweet counter, so de Silva asked him to fetch the manager.

'How can I help you, Inspector?' the manager asked when he arrived. 'If you want to have a look around, I think you will find everything is in order.'

'Thank you, but that's not the reason I'm here. I understand that a man named Johannes works for you. Is he here today? If so, I'd like to speak with him.'

'I'm afraid he's not. In fact, I haven't seen him for several days. He does the occasional odd job around the place for me and comes and goes as he pleases. He's not in any kind of trouble, is he?'

De Silva avoided the question. 'I believe he may be able to give me information relating to an inquiry I'm pursuing. Possibly you too can help me. What kind of man is this Johannes?'

The manager grinned. 'He wasn't first in the queue when they handed out brains, but he's strong and obliging enough if you know how to handle him.'

'How old would you say he is?'

'Hard to say. Nearing fifty perhaps.'

'And his appearance?'

'Tall and heavily built with a lot of pepper and salt coloured hair.'

De Silva showed him the photograph of Romesh. 'Do you recognise this man?'

The manager studied the photograph, eventually nodding. 'I've seen him before. He's friendly with Johannes, but that's all I can tell you about him.' He handed back the photograph. 'Why are you interested in him?'

Swiftly, de Silva brought out the story of an accident that he had concocted in case he needed it for the stall-holder. This time he went into more detail about how he hoped Johannes would be able to throw light on Romesh's circumstances so that his family could be traced.

'It's possible, but as I said, Johannes comes and goes.'

'If he returns, I'd be obliged if you'd call the police station.'

'Very well.'

'Incidentally, do you have any idea how he and Romesh know each other?'

'No, and I've told Johannes it's best to have nothing to do with him. I've never liked the man – shifty eyes. If I see him loitering by that counter over there,' he pointed to the cigarette and sweet counter, 'I always make sure he knows I'm looking, or I'd lay money on it that a few packets of cigarettes would disappear into his pocket.'

'I see. Well, thank you for your time. I hope to hear from you.'

* * *

Mulling over what he'd learnt, de Silva walked back to the Morris. So far, it seemed that Romesh hadn't found favour with anyone apart from his wife.

The manager's remarks about Johannes had given the impression that he would be easily led. A simple, trusting soul might be useful to a man like Romesh. If he'd had anything to do with the kidnappings and the murder of Marie O'Halloran, had he made use of Johannes? He could have provided Romesh with a conveniently empty house where the so-called séance could be held.

But were the crimes far too sophisticated for a man like Romesh to carry them out? Would he have the resources to set the scene for the abduction of Phoebe Tankerton, let alone access to the Residence to snatch Marie O'Halloran? Was he the writer of the letters to O'Halloran? Had he followed the O'Hallorans around India? Surely not. If he was involved, it must be as an accomplice. As de Silva reached Ridgeway Road, he was still debating whether he was barking up the wrong tree in any case.

Slipping in by the back entrance to the second house, he found Prasanna on watch. Unshaven, he looked weary, and de Silva felt sorry for him, although it would do the lad no harm to be reminded that much police work was painstaking and tedious rather than glamorous. He noticed some containers of rice, noodles, and fried snacks, as well as several rounds of paratha bread, and a box of fruit. Someone, presumably Prasanna's wife, Kuveni, had made sure that at least he wasn't going hungry.

'Nothing to report, I suppose.'

'No sir, no one's been here. The only company I've had has been rats and mice. The place is full of them.'

'I'll go and see how Nadar's getting on. Hopefully, we won't have to wait much longer for our man. I've found out more about him now.'

He explained what he had learnt from the cinema manager. 'He's a strong fellow, apparently, but you'll have the advantage of surprise,' he finished.

'Yes, sir.' Prasanna didn't look entirely convinced.

Next door, Nadar had nothing to add, so de Silva returned to the Morris and drove home to Sunnybank.

Jane was waiting for him in the drawing room, her embroidery in her lap. His favourite armchair looked inviting; the soft light from the table lamps made the colours of the room glow, and an arrangement of fiery orange canna lilies brightened the grate. After the bleak houses where he had left Prasanna and Nadar on duty, the peaceful domestic scene cheered him.

'Ah, here you are, dear,' said Jane. 'Dinner will be ready soon.'

Going to the sideboard, de Silva poured himself a whisky. 'Will you have something?'

'A small sherry would be nice. Then sit down and tell me what you found out this afternoon.'

He brought the glasses over, sat down and went over what the cinema manager had told him.

Jane frowned. 'So, given what the clerk at the Town Hall said and the age the cinema manager estimates Johannes to be now, when the de Grootes left Nuala, he might well have been just a little boy. How dreadful to have left him behind to fend for himself.'

De Silva took a swallow of whisky and felt its peaty warmth slip down his throat. 'I'm afraid he may have been someone the family preferred to forget.'

'Do you mean he was an illegitimate child?'

De Silva nodded. 'I fear he wouldn't be the first one to be left behind when colonial families left for England.'

The telephone rang in the hall and a servant answered then came to fetch him. 'Mr Frobisher from the Residence wishes to speak with you, sahib.'

De Silva drained his glass and stood up. 'I expect the boss wants an update. At least I have something to tell him.'

Frobisher listened as de Silva recounted the day's events. 'I'll pass all this on to the boss,' he said when de Silva came to the end. He paused. 'Actually, there's a couple of reasons I called. Firstly, we've been thinking about who is going to deliver the ransom money for poor Phoebe. Hank O'Halloran was keen to do it. Understandably, he feels very responsible, but the Tankertons thought it was asking too much of him. They've compromised on O'Halloran's secretary.'

'Has there been any more information about where the money is to be handed over?'

'That's the other thing. There's been no change. We're still waiting to hear tomorrow.'

De Silva heard a rueful sigh at the other end of the telephone. 'If this hadn't come up, I'd have been on leave, climbing in the Himalayas by now.'

Even the thought of those towering mountains made de Silva's head spin. Give him green valleys and sun-dappled beaches any day. It didn't matter how often people told you that a path was safe, and that others would be careful on your account; if that path snaked along a precipitous hillside, it wasn't the carelessness of others or one's own inattention that one feared, it was the almost irresistible compulsion to launch oneself into the void. The seductive pull of feet that seemed determined to ignore the brain's warnings: the self-destructive urge to jump. He dragged his thoughts back to what Frobisher was saying about the second thing – the wisdom of stationing more men at Ridgeway Road.

'If this Johannes comes back,' said Frobisher, 'we don't want him giving us the slip, or he might never return. Rather than call in reinforcements from Hatton or Kandy, which might take longer than we have in any case, what do you say to my lending a hand?'

'That's a very kind offer but, if you don't mind, I'd prefer you to be keeping an eye on Patterson, particularly as my men are at Ridgeway Road. I agree we are rather short on resources, but we'll cope. I can always join my men for a night or two.'

'Very well, if you're sure.'

* * *

'With Frobisher keeping an eye on Patterson, I have to show an example, even if it means spending an uncomfortable night for the sake of the case,' de Silva explained to Jane when he returned to the drawing room.

'Oh dear, I suppose it is for the best, but you will be careful, won't you?'

'Naturally.'

'And you must wrap up warmly.'

There was no fear of him forgetting to do that. Even in Ceylon's hot climate, it wasn't unknown for temperatures to plummet at night, particularly in the Hill Country.

'Will you be taking the Morris?' asked Jane.

'Just to the police station. Rather than going on to Ridgeway Road by car and risk causing comment, I should go by rickshaw.'

'That sounds very sensible.'

She stood up. 'I'll come and help you find some suitable clothes.'

CHAPTER 22

Prasanna and Nadar were surprised, but obviously glad, to see him.

After a brief word, de Silva instructed them to stand guard in the second house but take it in turns to sleep. He would remain in the house where the kidnapping had taken place. He decided to base himself on the middle floor so as to be best positioned to cover the floors above and below.

He took up his position and set down the kitbag he had brought with him. Looking around the room, he went over to the table that was the only piece of furniture. It was very dusty, but in the middle, there was a circle of cleaner wood. He was sure something had been removed, and not long ago. Perhaps Romesh got money by taking things belonging to the house and selling them. If Johannes looked on him as a friend, it might have been easy to make up a story of hardship.

It was going to be a long cold night and he was determined to stay awake. He blew on his hands and rubbed them together. The temperature was already dropping, and the chill emptiness of the house didn't help. He remembered that Jane had pressed upon him a hip flask of whisky. He pulled it from his bag and removed the cap. He had to remain alert, but a small swig worked wonders, the fiery liquid warming him up nicely.

As he waited, his mind turned to the following day, the

day when the Tankertons were due to pay the ransom and hopefully, not long after that, get their daughter back. He remembered that it was O'Halloran's secretary who had been nominated for the task. De Silva thought of the cool, efficient Miss Godley. Yes, she was someone who would perform it capably.

After staying in the same position for a couple of hours, he felt the need to shake the cramp from his legs. Checking for any unusual sounds and hearing none, he got up and took a walk around the house, still always careful to tread quietly and shield the beam of his torch with his cupped hand in case Johannes was close by. As he went into each room, he heard the scamper of tiny feet and choruses of indignant squeaks. The rodent population was about its nightly business.

At the front of the building he no longer needed his torch, for the moon was up, bathing the rooms in eerie light. To his sleepy imagination, the ghosts of people who had lived in them drifted in the chilly air: the warm blood that had once run in their veins frozen for ever. He thought of a poem by Keats that Jane loved. It was entitled *Saint Agnes Eve*. The opening lines came back to him.

Saint Agnes Eve, ah, bitter chill it was,
The owl for all his feathers was a'cold,
The hare limped trembling through—

He held his breath; there was a sound on the landing. The sound of someone approaching the room where de Silva was standing. Stealthily, he moved to the side of the door so that he would be behind it as it opened. In the stillness, the creak sounded like the cracking of centuries-old ice.

Unaware of de Silva's presence, the man who entered the room crossed to where a few old clothes lay on the floor. He tugged a tattered jersey over his head and then shook free his wild mane of greying hair. The jersey stretched tightly over his barrel chest. His face was broad with high cheekbones and pale eyes, and his skin was much lighter than de Silva's. Was that because Dutch blood mingled with Ceylonese in his veins?

De Silva took a step out from behind the door. He must be careful; he didn't want to alarm the fellow. It was important to get him to talk. 'Are you Johannes?' he asked quietly.

The man swung round. His eyes widened and his head went up. He reminded de Silva of a deer scenting danger. In a flash, he barged de Silva aside with his shoulder and ran for the door. Knocked sideways, de Silva struggled to regain his balance.

Shouting for Prasanna and Nadar, he stumbled after the man. Surprisingly fast on his feet for a big fellow, the fugitive was already halfway to the top floor landing. Presumably, he'd returned to the house by the front door, but assumed in his panic that it wasn't the safest way out again.

De Silva's heart raced as he struggled to catch up and saw the man disappear into the room where the séance had been held. On the threshold, he was just in time to see him race into the other room and then the passage. His chest burning, de Silva doubled over. He needed to catch his breath. Prasanna and Nadar ought to be able to stop him. He'd made enough noise on the bare wooden floors as he ran from de Silva.

All at once, he heard shouting and a crash: then silence. He listened intently and prayed that Prasanna and Nadar had got their man. As he emerged from the passage into the second house, de Silva breathed a huge sigh of relief. Pinned with his face to the wall, the fugitive was going nowhere. He had run straight into a punch delivered by the strong bowling arm of Sergeant Prasanna.

CHAPTER 23

They lit the candles in the room where the séance had taken place, each identified themselves as Nuala policemen, then questioned Johannes there. It was a slow process, but eventually it became apparent that, unless the story they prised out of the frightened man was a pack of lies, he had been duped by the unknown lady whose existence de Silva had learnt of at the Town Hall into taking part in what would turn out to be Phoebe's kidnap. The lady had offered money for the use of the houses in Ridgeway Road. She asked if Johannes could find someone to help him and he involved Romesh. She had claimed that she wanted to set up a surprise for a friend.

'What kind of a surprise?' asked de Silva.

'Her friend wanted to have her fortune told.'

'Did this lady have a name?'

'I don't remember.'

'What did she look like?'

'A white lady. A Britisher.'

'You must be able to tell us more than that.'

A mulish look came over Johannes's face; his lips clamped shut.

De Silva sighed. This was going to take a long time, and time was something they didn't have much of. 'She told you a pack of lies, didn't she? What she really wanted to do was capture the young woman she called a friend and lock her up against her will. Even if you weren't aware of that at the beginning, I don't think you believed the story for long.'

Johannes tried to jump up from the chair they had sat him in, but Prasanna, who stood behind him, put a restraining hand on his shoulder. Johannes began to whimper.

'You know you've done wrong, don't you,' said de Silva sternly. 'It will be best for you if you tell us everything, then we may be able to help you. Has this lady already given you money?'

If the fellow still had it, he thought, there was an outside chance of tracing her through the numbers on the bank notes.

'She said she would soon. There was going to be a lot of money, and she might take me with her when she went back to her own country. She could see I was a gentleman.'

So she had played on Johannes's obsession.

Johannes's voice faded, and he started to shake. De Silva was afraid that he might collapse but pressed on, nonetheless. 'And were you involved in a recent incident at the Residence involving another young lady, an American? Were Romesh or the British lady involved in that matter?'

There was a long pause then Johannes rallied. 'I don't know anything. I didn't do no harm. Romesh said we weren't doing anything wrong.'

He bowed his head. De Silva was certain that Romesh had understood exactly what was going on and had been a far more active accomplice, most likely in the kidnap of both Marie and Phoebe. He also had no doubt Johannes was lying.

'Are you afraid?' he asked.

Johannes nodded.

'Of the lady who asked you to help her?'

'Yes.' He spoke so quietly that his voice was almost inaudible. He gave de Silva a beseeching look.

'Tell us what happened,' repeated de Silva. 'If you do, we'll make sure she doesn't come near you.'

There was a long pause as fear, trust, and indecision warred on Johannes's face.

'The lady with the red hair,' he said at last. 'The younger one. When we saw her, she was on the floor.'

'Was the older lady you met, the British lady, with her?' Johannes nodded.

'Was she still dressed in European clothes?'

'No, she was dressed like a fortune teller with a dark face. But I knew it was her. She had the same British accent.'

'When did you first see the young lady with the red hair?'

'After we moved the mirror away.'

So Johannes may not have seen O'Halloran being knocked out.

'Was Romesh with you?'

'Yes.'

So, presumably, they moved the mirror away from the hole to the room next door from behind it. 'Go on.'

'The lady said me and Romesh had to carry the young lady away.'

'Where did you take her?'

Johannes shrank back into himself. 'I don't know.'

'Sir, we're not getting anywhere with this fellow. Can't we arrest him and take him down to the station now?' asked Prasanna.

De Silva silenced him with a wave of the hand, keeping his attention on Johannes. 'Your friend Romesh is dead,' he said quietly. 'Do you understand me? Dead. My guess is that you were not involved, but I must warn you that if the lady who asked for your help finds you, she'll very likely kill you.'

His eyes wild with terror, Johannes jumped up and tried to run for the door, but Prasanna was too quick for him.

'If you want our help, you must tell us everything you know,' said de Silva, when the man had been hauled back and pushed, none too gently, in his chair. 'What was the lady's name?'

'She said it was Patterson,' whispered Johannes.

De Silva frowned. He wondered if she was telling the truth. If she was related to Patterson in some way, where had she been all the time that he'd been travelling with the Tankertons?

'What did she look like?'

Johannes's expression turned sullen again; he curled in on himself. 'I can't remember.'

De Silva wasn't sure whether this lapse of memory was genuine, or whether Johannes was still afraid of the consequences of saying too much. If he was putting on an act, it was a very persistent one. So far, they had established that Johannes and Romesh had been involved in Phoebe Tankerton's kidnap. Most likely Romesh had been killed by, or on the orders of, the British lady who was involved in it. It was also established that she had disguised herself as the medium. They had been so close to her, thought de Silva grimly. So close, not just to Phoebe's abductor but also, perhaps, to Marie's murderer as well.

'Where was the young lady taken, Johannes?'

'I don't know. Romesh went with her.'

That might be true, as Johannes had returned to the house. Exasperation twisted in de Silva's gut. Through the window, he saw that dawn was coming up, streaking the sky with pink and gold.

'Let's get him back to the station. It's time we reported to the boss.'

CHAPTER 24

Back at the station, de Silva formally arrested Johannes for the kidnapping of Phoebe Tankerton. Adding charges relating to Marie's disappearance and death might come later. He left Prasanna and Nadar in charge and went up to the Residence to report to Archie. As on de Silva's previous visit, he noticed that a subdued air hung over the place. Secretaries and officials passing through the reception hall spoke in low voices, and no one smiled.

'Come in!'

Archie's voice boomed through the door in answer to the servant's knock. De Silva went in to find his boss at his desk, a glum expression on his face. 'I hope you're bringing me good news. It's been one damn thing after another. It was O'Halloran's wish to have his daughter cremated and her ashes were interred this morning. The vicar conducted the service as best as he could, but inevitably, it was a distressing occasion. Late last night, Walter Tankerton was taken ill, and Hebden had to be called up in a hurry. He said it was a minor stroke. Lucky it wasn't worse.'

'I'm very sorry to hear it,' said de Silva. 'How is Mrs Tankerton?'

'Bearing up remarkably well. There's a surprising amount of steel under that quiet exterior. Hebden arranged for Tankerton to be taken down to Kandy. The hospital there is better able to care for him than we are here, but she refuses to leave her post until her daughter's safely back with her.'

Archie took a cigarette out of the packet of Passing Clouds on his desk, lit up and inhaled deeply. 'Well, get on with what you came to say.'

He listened while de Silva ran through the details of the interview with Johannes. When he had finished, silence descended for a few moments, broken only by the tick of the grandfather clock in the corner and Darcy's stentorian breathing. Oh, to be a pet dog, thought de Silva, with nothing to worry about apart from when the next walk or biscuit would come one's way.

'This fellow Johannes,' said Archie at last. 'It may be worth returning him to the Ridgeway Road house to use as bait, but we might let a bit of time elapse first. For the moment, we need to concentrate on Phoebe Tankerton. We've got the instructions as to where the money should be taken now.'

'Where, sir?'

'The temple on the edge of town. The particular shrine it's to be left at is specified and the way the parcel is to be hidden among the offerings. Hank O'Halloran's secretary's ready to go this afternoon.'

De Silva's brow furrowed. 'There'll be a lot of people at the temple at that time. It will be hard to watch to see who collects the parcel.'

'Grace Tankerton's in charge now, and she still insists there's to be no attempt to do so. We'll have to wait to pick up Patterson until Phoebe's returned. If this woman who played the part of the medium's called Patterson, it's another piece of evidence against him.'

Or it might be a lie and merely evidence that the lady was amusing herself at their expense, thought de Silva. But then why would she suspect they were onto Patterson? Was it plausible that the name was just a coincidence?

'Has there been any news from Scotland Yard about Mr Patterson, sir?' he asked.

Archie regarded him wearily. 'Not yet, I'm afraid. Is there anything else?'

'It occurs to me that Miss Tankerton may not have been taken far, sir.'

'Why do you think that?'

'If we're right that Romesh was killed by, or on the orders of, the lady impersonating the medium, it's interesting that the murder took place at his house. We know from Johannes that Romesh was in charge of guarding her. If he was keeping her at a place far from home, why was he at his house on the night when he was murdered?'

Archie massaged his chin with a thumb and forefinger. 'Good point. But I'm nervous about going against Mrs Tankerton and searching Romesh's house. What if we put the wind up the kidnappers?'

An idea flashed into de Silva's mind. 'How about my wife going, sir? She could do so on the pretext of visiting Romesh's widow. I have a message for her anyway from the Crown Hotel.'

'But won't it raise suspicions if Mrs de Silva looks around and asks questions about the place?'

'She will not be the one looking, sir. I'll tell my sergeant to wear plain clothes and take her there by rickshaw. While he is waiting to bring her back, he will have time to try and find something out.'

Archie pondered for a few moments. 'Very well,' he said at last. 'But tell him to be extremely cautious. Does he know how to drive a rickshaw?'

De Silva grinned. 'If not, he will soon learn.'

'Will Mrs de Silva agree?'

'I think so.'

'Good, then we have a plan.'

* * *

A gleam came into Jane's eyes when he returned to Sunny-bank and, having told her about the night's events, put the proposition to her.

'Of course I'll go,' she said. 'Perhaps I'll take Emerald with me. With two of us there, it might be less suspicious. We'll simply be two ladies from a local charity coming to visit this poor widow. We have your message from Sanjeewa Gunesekera to give her, and while we're in the house, Prasanna can carry out his part of the plan.'

'Thank you, my love. You will be careful, won't you?'

'Of course. I promise I'll make sure that no one suspects a thing. What's going to happen to Johannes?'

De Silva pondered for a few moments. 'I'm not sure at present. We know he was in on the plot to kidnap Phoebe, and it seems likely he and Romesh were involved in Marie's kidnap too. But it doesn't automatically follow that he killed, or helped to kill, Marie. At some point we'll have to see if O'Halloran recognises him as being at the clearing when Marie was shot. We might even want to see Johannes's reaction if we give him a sight of Patterson. But his main use to us now is as a way of finding the people at the heart of the crimes, and we need to keep his arrest quiet for fear of tipping them off.'

He scratched his head. 'I wish I knew whether he's genuinely unable to remember all the details as he claims or is just being slippery.'

'It might be the former. I've read that fear does some-times blot out memories, and you say Johannes is far from being mentally robust in the first place. Rather than face what happened and the danger he may be in, he may have buried a lot of what happened deep inside.'

'Hmm. Anyway, I'd better go back to the station and get Prasanna under orders. We only have a few hours before the money's due to be handed over. If, by some miracle, the two of you manage to find Phoebe before the money needs to be handed over, the Tankertons will be very happy and no less rich than they are now.'

* * *

He hadn't slept the previous night, and his eyes felt heavy with exhaustion, but a nap would have to wait. As he drove, he thought about Patterson. To be on the safe side, he'd need to be detained as soon as Phoebe was returned. But they still had no evidence against him apart from the business card, Johannes being told that the bogus medium's name was Patterson, and the fact that he was the most likely suspect out of the people who had been aware that Phoebe was going to visit the medium.

It would be interesting to know whether Patterson had any money apart from what the Tankertons were paying him. The ransom money was an enormous sum. It wouldn't be easy to hide. It might be possible for Archie to make enquiries of the British banks in Colombo and further afield to see if Patterson had deposited any large amounts of cash. On the other hand, he might be too clever to fall into that trap.

At the station, he gave Prasanna his instructions then checked on Johannes. He was snoring in his cell. For once, de Silva envied him.

Then it occurred to him that while Jane was visiting Romesh's widow, there was something useful he could do. There was a new avenue of inquiry that he hadn't pursued yet. It might lead nowhere, but he never liked to leave a stone unturned. But first, he had better put on civilian clothes.

He went to the Crown Hotel where he found that his friend Sanjeewa was off duty. Leaving a request for some information, he returned to the Morris and drove to the temple on the edge of town.

CHAPTER 25

With Prasanna gamely pedalling the rickshaw, Jane and Emerald leant back in the passenger seat.

'We'll have to give him as much time as possible,' said Emerald. 'If we're offered tea, we must accept.'

'I don't know that the poor woman will be in a state to receive visitors. We may have difficulty staying for much longer than it takes to deliver our message. I suppose we could wander around the bazaar for a while afterwards. Would you mind doing that if Prasanna isn't with us?'

'Not at all. I'm sure we'll be perfectly safe in the middle of the day.'

In fact, the house where Romesh's widow was staying was busy with well-wishers bringing all kinds of food from naan bread and fruit to bowls of soft cheese and baskets of eggs. In the cramped, steamy kitchen area, large pots of rice and vegetable curry bubbled on the blackened, wood-burning stove, filling the air with enticing aromas. In the midst of it all, Achala looked bemused, her eyes red from weeping. Jane pitied her. Whatever crimes her husband had committed, it was hard to believe this hard-working woman had taken any part in them.

They gave her the news that she need not go to the Crown until she was feeling up to it, but she would be paid. They also explained that nothing was now preventing her husband's funeral and cremation, and she could return home whenever she wished.

'Do you think we've given Prasanna long enough?' whispered Emerald after they had accepted and drunk the cups of tea offered by some of Achala's female relations.

'I hope so. I don't think we can stay any longer.'

In the lane outside, Prasanna was waiting by the rickshaw. Jane noticed a small boy nearby who watched them attentively as they approached.

'Did you have any luck?' she asked Prasanna quietly.

He nodded towards the boy. 'He showed me an outhouse at the back of the building. Apparently, a poor family lived in it once, but a few years ago, there was a fire, and since then, no one has used it because it's unsafe. The boy claims he saw someone arrive by car and go in there the night before last. He says he has more to tell, but he wants money first.'

Jane looked in her purse. 'Tell him to follow us. We'll stop a few streets away and speak there.'

Prasanna pedalled slowly as they set off, but the boy followed along at a good pace, so he soon speeded up. When they had put a reasonable distance between themselves and the house where Romesh's widow was staying, Jane called out to Prasanna to stop. The boy came trotting up, and she gave him a rupee. 'There will be two more for you if what you have to tell us is useful.'

The boy nodded.

He spoke in a mixture of Tamil and English, and frequently, Jane had to ask Prasanna to translate, but the gist of his story was that he had seen a lady in a burka leave the outhouse, then go into Romesh's building. Later, she returned to the outhouse and after a while, came out with another person, got into the car and drove away.

'Ask him if this other person seemed willing to go,' said Emerald.

The boy answered the question rapidly.

'He says the other person seemed drunk,' said Prasanna. 'They had to be dragged along.'

'Does he think it was a lady or a man?'

'A lady,' said Prasanna after another exchange.

Seemingly having no more to tell them, the boy held out a grubby hand for his two rupees and Jane gave them to him. As the rickshaw jolted away, she sighed. 'I'm afraid we're too late. If it was Phoebe Tankerton in that outhouse, she's been moved.'

CHAPTER 26

De Silva paused at the door of the temple to allow his eyes time to become accustomed to the dim light. In an hour or so, it would be lit by thousands of candles and packed with people coming to venerate the holy relic, but for the moment, it was quiet.

Going to the left, he found the place where the ransom money was to be deposited. For a few moments, he stood before the brass statue of the seated buddha with his head bowed in prayer. Afterwards, he studied the offerings on the altar, where bowls made of metal or clay were heaped with brightly coloured flowers and sticky sweetmeats. When he had satisfied himself that he would remember how everything was arranged, he walked back to the Morris and drove home.

* * *

'I wish I had better news for you,' said Jane sadly. 'The more I think about it, the more I feel sure Phoebe was there, and that the lady the boy saw moved her. If only we'd gone sooner, we might have found her.'

'Police work has many "if onlys", my love,' said de Silva.

Jane looked at him curiously. 'You don't seem very disappointed.'

'We must take the rough with the smooth. As long as

Phoebe is safe, there will be no harm done in that respect. Although I hope we can then find out who this lady is. It seems to me that she will be a prime suspect for Romesh's murder.'

He glanced at the drawing room clock. 'Laura Godley will be depositing the ransom money about now.'

'Let's hope the kidnappers give poor Phoebe back quickly once they have it.' Jane shivered. 'Shanti, you don't think anything will go wrong this time, do you? How awful if they don't keep their word.'

'I think they will keep it.'

'How can you be sure when they killed poor Marie O'Halloran?'

'Something tells me that this time is different.'

After dinner, they sat in the drawing room. Jane jumped and nearly dropped her sewing when the telephone rang, but it was only Emerald asking if they'd heard anything. Two more hours passed, and they were about to give up and go to bed when it rang again. De Silva returned to the drawing room beaming.

'She's safe!'

He felt as if a heavy burden had been lifted from his shoulders.

'A message came that she was at the Nuala caves. Archie sent Frobisher straight up there with a party of servants, and they found her. She was cold and very frightened; hungry too. She said she'd been alone for some time, but with it being impossible to tell day from night in the caves, she wasn't sure exactly how long.'

The Nuala caves were believed to have been inhabited long ago, and people sometimes visited them to see what remained of the ancient wall paintings, but visits were infrequent, and much of the cave system saw no visitors from one year's end to the next. It was a clever place to have hidden Phoebe Tankerton.

'Oh thank goodness.' Jane wiped a tear from her eye. 'Her parents must be so relieved.'

'I'm not sure Walter knows yet. He's still in hospital at Kandy. But according to Florence, Grace Tankerton's so overjoyed, she's hardly able to speak. Florence said that the reunion between her and her daughter was very affecting. Archie thinks it tactful to allow the Tankertons a little time together before asking Phoebe any questions, and Phoebe needs to sleep, but he wants me up at the Residence first thing in the morning.'

CHAPTER 27

On his arrival at the Residence after breakfast the next morning, de Silva was pleased to find that Phoebe Tankerton appeared to be recovering well from her ordeal. With her mother in attendance, she met de Silva and Archie in his study. De Silva was impressed by how much kinder to her mother she was, allowing her to hold her hand throughout the interview. Grace Tankerton looked far happier and less careworn than de Silva had ever seen her.

'I'm afraid I don't have much to tell you,' Phoebe said. 'Everything happened so quickly, and it was very dark when we were in Madame Batavi's apartment. We had been offered tea, but I didn't want any as I only like coffee. Shortly after drinking his tea, Hank started acting and talking strangely, then he fell. I went over to help him – we had been on opposite sides of the table. When he didn't seem able to get up, I began to feel scared. The next I knew, I was grabbed from behind, and a cloth was pressed over my mouth and nose. There was the same horrible smell I remembered from the evening when Marie was kidnapped at the Residence. My heart started to beat very fast and I felt terribly dizzy.'

Her voice broke, and she was silent for a few moments, her head resting on her mother's shoulder. Grace Tankerton stroked her hair.

Phoebe took a deep breath and rallied. 'I passed out.

When I came to, I was tied up, and whatever I was in – some kind of van or lorry – was moving. The road it was on must have been very bumpy because I kept rolling into things. It was hard to see in the darkness, but they felt like wooden crates. From the smell, they might have contained fruit.'

'Were you alone?'

Phoebe nodded. 'I'm not sure where Madame Batavi had got to, or Hank. I was so relieved when Mother told me he hadn't come to any serious harm. I hope I can see him soon,' she added.

Her mother squeezed her hand. 'All in good time, my love.'

'Did you see Madame Batavi again after you were taken from the house?'

Phoebe shook her head. 'There were two men with me when the van stopped, both of them masked. One of them seemed to be in charge. The other one did what he was told to do. They put a blindfold on me, so I didn't see the place they took me to until we were inside. Only one of them was with me then. I don't know what happened to the other one.'

De Silva guessed that Romesh had dismissed Johannes when he was no longer useful. He wondered if Romesh had hoped to keep all the money for himself. Alternatively, Johannes had been overwhelmed and frightened by the situation he found himself in and run away.

'Is there anything you remember about the place? Any distinguishing features?' asked Archie.

Phoebe thought briefly. 'It was dark and very dirty. There was a smell of damp, and I think there must have been a fire there once because the ceiling and the walls were all blackened. There was no proper window, just a slit in one wall.'

It sounded like the outhouse Prasanna had found, thought de Silva.

'I spent a night there, but the next night, a woman came and took me away. She wore a burka, so I never saw her face.'

The wearing of a burka agreed with the story that the boy Prasanna found had told. De Silva had a strong suspicion this woman was the same one who had played the part of the medium.

'She spoke with an odd accent that I couldn't place,' added Phoebe. 'I wondered whether she was putting it on.'

'Thank you, my dear,' said Archie. 'That's enough for now, don't you agree, Inspector?' He gave de Silva a meaningful look.

'Of course,' de Silva said quickly. 'But should you remember anything that might help the investigation, Miss Tankerton, I'd be grateful if you'd speak to Mr Clutterbuck or myself straight away.'

'Of course, Inspector,' answered Grace Tankerton for her daughter. 'Now, since you have no more questions, I'd like Phoebe to rest. In a few days' time, I'll be taking her down to Kandy. My husband's been informed she's safe, but I know how much he's longing to see her.'

'Of course, ma'am,' said Archie. 'And if you need any assistance making the arrangements, you only need to ask.'

More pressure, thought de Silva. A decision on what to do about Andrew Patterson couldn't be put off much longer.

CHAPTER 28

After de Silva had left for the Residence, Jane rang the bell
for one of the servants to clear the breakfast things and
then went to the drawing room. Deeply relieved that the
Tankertons' daughter had been recovered, she had to admit
to herself that a feeling of disquiet remained. It was very
likely the kidnappers would get away with their crime, and
that offended her sense of justice, but more importantly,
it gave them the chance to strike again. There were other
wealthy families in Ceylon – owners of large tea planta-
tions, or families who controlled the gemstone market for
which Ceylon was well known. Despite the fact that Phoebe Tankerton was back with her mother, Jane was sure that
de Silva too would have preferred it to be in circumstances
where the criminals had been locked up, rather than leaving
them at large.

Unusually for her, she had no plans for the rest of the
day and fell to wondering how to pass the time. She wasn't
in the mood for sewing or embroidery and she'd written up
her household accounts a few days ago. Briefly, she debated
whether to make a start on her library books. There was
a new Agatha Christie she was looking forward to, but
perhaps she would finish off a little job first. There were still
a few old magazines she hadn't sorted through.

Half of them were Shanti's gardening ones and didn't
take long to deal with. Her film magazines took more time,

as she enjoyed being reminded of films she'd seen and the goings-on in the film world.

After a while, she came to an article about one of her favourite stars that she didn't remember reading, so she settled down to enjoy it. One of the photographs showed him with a group of other actors who had taken part in one of his most famous films. A young man in the front row made her pause. He was handsome, with a strong nose and roguish eyes; his smile reminded her of someone. For a few moments, she racked her brains, but the name eluded her. It wasn't important, probably nothing more than a vague resemblance, but it always irritated her when her memory let her down.

She put the magazine aside on the pile of those to be given away. This time, she might offer them to Emerald. Her friend always said that a fresh supply of magazines was welcome to give patients something to read while they waited for their appointments at Doctor Hebden's clinic.

When she had finished looking through the rest of the magazines, she took them all out to the hall and left them on the side table. Perhaps she would make a start on the Agatha Christie after all.

The sun had moved round and the verandah was in shade. She settled down to read and was just finishing the first chapter when she felt something rub against her calf. Looking down, she smiled.

'This is the third time in a week. What am I to do with you?'

A plaintive meow emitted from the black and white kitten gazing up at her with beseeching eyes. Soon, her companion appeared, weaving his way through the legs of the wicker table to the side of Jane's chair. With one bound, he jumped onto the railing that divided the verandah from the garden, balanced on its narrow, wooden top and proceeded to wash his paws with his small pink tongue.

'I suppose you're hoping for milk,' said Jane to the kitten

that had remained at her side. She reached to stroke its soft, sleek head and smiled. 'I don't know what Shanti will say.'

But some feline company might do them both good. She had grown up with animals, and hadn't Shanti told her how fond he'd been of the pet mongoose and the mynah bird he'd had as a little boy?

The servants were all busy, so she went to the kitchen, found two saucers and filled them with milk from the cool pantry. Back on the verandah, the kittens' tails shot up when they saw her coming. She put the saucers on the floor and immediately they ran to lap up the milk. After they had cleared away every drop, they curled up at the top of the steps to the garden and went to sleep. Smiling, Jane watched them as their little bodies rose and fell. It would be cruel to drive them away.

CHAPTER 29

'Take a turn with me around the garden,' said Archie when the Tankertons had left them. De Silva nodded. No doubt Archie wanted to speak to him about Andrew Patterson. If the Tankertons left for Kandy, it was likely he would go with them.

As they started out down the path towards the tennis courts, his guess proved right. Archie squinted into the sunshine. 'Well, if we're going to arrest Patterson, it's time we got on with it. Do you agree?'

De Silva frowned; he had been thinking more about the situation with Patterson. 'I'm not so sure, sir. All our evidence is circumstantial. If we arrest him, he's bound to deny he took any part in the crimes. When he goes down to Kandy with the Tankertons, I'd prefer to ask the police at Kandy to watch him for us.'

'To what purpose?'

'So that he can be arrested if we uncover direct evidence up here that leads us to him.'

Archie ruminated for a while then nodded. 'Very well. Let's hope we don't have to wait much longer to hear from Scotland Yard. I've told Frobisher to ginger them up. I'll ask him how he's got on. You speak to the relevant people at Kandy, and I'll have a word with William Petrie. He wanted to be kept informed of what's going on in any case.'

He grimaced. 'But I fear that at the moment, he has

other things on his mind. The news from England's giving increasing cause for concern. Last year, Mr Chamberlain spoke of peace in our time, but if Hitler attempts to take over any more territory, peace may not prevail. England and France have given assurances that they'll support the Poles if Hitler encroaches on their borders. If he does, we'll have to make good on that promise, or the British empire will be a laughing-stock.'

To say nothing of the plight of the Polish people, thought de Silva. But with Archie's background, he would inevitably see the issue from the British angle.

'Still, we have our more immediate problem to deal with,' Archie added briskly. 'Let me know what you arrange with Kandy. Perversely, it's just as well that Walter Tankerton isn't well enough to travel, or so I hear. With luck, Patterson will stay in Kandy with them, and we won't be forced into a difficult decision just yet.'

On his way out from the Residence, de Silva decided to go straight to the station and telephone Kandy. He was still mulling over what he would say when he drew up there. In the public room, Nadar greeted him.

'Anything to report, Constable?'

'Only that a gentleman came in asking for you, sir.'

'Did he leave his name?'

Nadar shook his head. 'I asked for it, but he just said he'd come back later today and left in a hurry.'

De Silva frowned. 'Odd. Did he give any indication of what he wanted to see me about?'

'I also asked that, sir, but he said he'd prefer to explain when he saw you.'

'Well, I expect to be here for the rest of the day, so if he comes back, we'll find out. I need a call to Kandy. Put one in for me, please. Ask for Inspector Weerasinghe or Inspector Chockalingham.'

'Right away, sir.'

In his office, he hung his cap on its hook and settled down at his desk to wait for the call to come through. It was Weerasinghe who came on the line, and he quickly understood what needed to be done. De Silva promised to let him know when Patterson and the Tankertons left Nuala and then ended the call.

Picking up a pen, he made a few notes of the morning's meeting with Archie then leant back, tapping the end of the pen against his chin. Was it worth questioning Johannes again? As Archie had instructed, the fellow was still in the cells. For a man like Johannes, who was used to living without the ties of people or possessions, it must be a strange experience. Still, it didn't do to lavish too much sympathy on him. Even if he was easily led and not too bright, he had admitted to taking part in at least one extremely serious crime and that seemed only the half of it.

The telephone rang and he picked up the receiver.

'It's Mr Frobisher from the Residence, sir,' said Nadar.

'Put him through.' There was a pause.

'Good afternoon, Mr Frobisher. Do you have news for me?'

'We've drawn a blank on Patterson, I'm afraid. Scotland Yard says he has a clean record. They were asked by an important prospective client to check him out when he set up his private security business just over two years ago. Indeed, his military career both during and after the war is a distinguished one. He left the army four years ago after he was injured in an accident involving a field gun. He receives an army pension, but it's probably not enough to live on. I've informed the boss.'

'Did he say much?'

'Just that it's as well you had reservations about arresting Patterson. We've probably avoided offending the Tankertons.'

De Silva thanked him and replaced the receiver. The news made his latest line of inquiry seem far more crucial than it had done previously. It was time he paid another visit to the temple.

CHAPTER 30

The temple was peaceful after the hubbub of the previous afternoon. Monks dressed in saffron robes went about their devotions on silent feet, and the aroma of incense filled the air. Dressed in civilian clothes, de Silva went to the shrine he had visited before and bowed his head once more before the statue of the buddha. When he had finished saying a short prayer, he raised his head and studied the bowls of offerings. He was almost certain that none of the arrangements of flowers and sweetmeats had been disturbed, although a few gifts had been added. If the package of ransom money had been there, surely Laura Godley would have taken the precaution of concealing it under some of the flowers and sweetmeats? There were two possibilities: she had been careless, or she hadn't left it there.

* * *

His mind racing, de Silva put his foot down as he drove back to the station. He would telephone the Crown straight away. Hopefully, Sanjeewa would be there with the information he'd asked for.

Nadar looked startled when he hurried into the public room. He wasn't used to seeing his boss move at anything much faster than a leisurely pace. 'Is something wrong, sir?'

'Get me the Crown Hotel. I need to speak to the deputy manager, Mr Gunesekera.'

'Shall I do that right now, sir?'

'Didn't I say so?'

'It's just that there's a gentleman waiting to see you.'

He pointed towards the door to the waiting room. It stood ajar and through it, de Silva saw a tall European dressed in a dark suit and a Homburg hat. He had grey hair and a moustache and wore horn-rimmed glasses. His appearance slowed de Silva in his tracks. It chimed with Sanjeewa's description of the man who had been asking for Hank O'Halloran at the Crown.

'What's his name?'

'It's Barnett, sir. Mr Aldous Barnett.'

'I'll go to my office. Show him in. When you've done that, call the Crown as I told you to. If Mr Gunesekera has found out for me which bank O'Halloran drew on to pay his hotel bill, take a note of the name.'

A moment or two passed before the door opened and Nadar showed Barnett in. De Silva rose from his chair. 'Good afternoon, Mr Barnett. How may I help you?'

Barnett looked at him keenly. 'I trust, Inspector, that we'll be able to help each other.' He spoke with an American accent.

'I'm looking for a man named Hank O'Halloran.'

Barnett sat down and snapped open the clasps of the black briefcase he'd placed in front of him. He brought out an official-looking piece of paper and handed it across the desk for de Silva to read.

'My credentials. As you'll see, I work for First Global Insurance Corporation of Philadelphia. My employers are keen to talk to Mr O'Halloran, or as he previously called himself before arriving in India, Harlan. I understand he's in town and was staying at the Crown Hotel, but they tell me he checked out. I'm hoping you can enlighten me as to his whereabouts.'

A jolt of excitement went through de Silva as he scanned the letter, but handing it back, he tried to keep his expression neutral. It was best not to divulge anything yet.

'Thank you, sir. All seems to be in order. May I ask why your employers want to talk to Mr O'Halloran?'

'We have reason to believe that while he was living in America, he put in a series of fraudulent insurance claims.'

De Silva's heartbeat quickened. Might this be the lead he'd been waiting for?

'Eventually, my employers became suspicious and asked for further particulars of the claims, a proportion of which had already been paid out. Harlan failed to provide the information and left town, leaving no forwarding address.'

'You say this man was called Harlan. How can you be sure that he's now calling himself O'Halloran?'

A dry smile did nothing to illuminate Barnett's face. 'Let's just say I'm good at my job, Inspector. First Global hire only the best. I've been after him for a long time and just missed unmasking him in Calcutta.'

De Silva wavered. This confident stranger's credentials looked convincing, but he had never heard of the company he claimed to work for. The wisest course would be to speak to Archie before disclosing where O'Halloran was.

'I may be able to help you, sir, but first, I'll need some more information.'

'If it's within my power.'

'Does this Mr Harlan have anyone travelling with him?'

'Only his wife, whom I'd also like to interview.'

That was interesting – his wife, not his secretary, and no Marie. 'Can you describe the lady for me?'

'In her early forties. Tall for a woman and striking. Dark hair.'

The description matched Laura Godley. With his suspicion that she hadn't left the ransom money at the shrine, and this new information, de Silva was increasingly inclined to believe that he was at last getting somewhere. With Patterson out of the picture, who else had known when Phoebe would be visiting Madame Batavi? Laura Godley, who had arranged the meeting, and O'Halloran himself. If Barnett was right and Marie wasn't O'Halloran's daughter, nor was Laura Godley his secretary, was the conclusion that she and O'Halloran had conspired to kidnap Phoebe and kill Marie? In that case, O'Halloran's story that he had been drugged and tied up to prevent him from protecting Phoebe was a lie. The motive for kidnapping Phoebe was simple enough: money. But why would they want Marie dead?

He pushed back his chair and stood up. 'I must ask you to give me a little time, sir. I need to speak with someone. But if you would be so kind as to leave details of where to find you with my constable, after that, I hope to be able to give you the help you require.'

CHAPTER 31

'Mr Gunesekera was still out, sir, but he's expected back soon,' said Nadar when de Silva followed Barnett to the public room. 'I left a message.'

'Thank you. Telephone the Residence for me, would you?' He shook Barnett's hand, still maintaining an imperturbable expression. 'Goodbye, sir. I'll be in touch.'

Barnett thanked him then gave Nadar the details of where to find him before leaving.

It was Charlie Frobisher who came on the line when one of the Residence's telephonists connected the call.

'I'm afraid you've been passed to me,' Frobisher said cheerfully. 'The boss is busy, and you know how he hates to be disturbed, but if it's urgent, I'll take the risk for you.'

'It is,' said de Silva.

'Can you elaborate?'

Swiftly, de Silva explained about Aldous Barnett's visit and what he'd had to say about Hank O'Halloran and his wife. A low whistle came from Charlie Frobisher's end of the line. 'This is a turn up for the book, and no mistake. And you say this chap Barnett's credentials seemed genuine?'

'The letter he showed me certainly looked to be.'

'First Global Insurance Corporation of Philadelphia,' mused Frobisher. 'I haven't heard of them, but one of my colleagues has recently returned from a posting in that part of the world. He should be able to tell me if they're reputable.

It would be good to have more than their respectability to put before the boss, though. Have you anything else?'

De Silva explained about the offerings at the shrine and the question he had asked Sanjeewa Gunesekera.

'Good thinking,' said Frobisher. 'If we know the bank, we can find out what's been happening on the account. It would be too soon for Phoebe's ransom money to have been paid in, but there should be a record of Marie's coming out. I'll wait for you to call me back before I tackle Archie.'

As he waited for Sanjeewa to telephone, de Silva's impatience almost got the better of him. Drumming his fingers on the desktop, he debated going up to the Crown. He was annoyed with himself that he hadn't thought to ask Archie to check with Scotland Yard to see if they had anything on file for O'Halloran as well as for Patterson. It might have put them onto him earlier.

The telephone ringing interrupted his thoughts.

'Ah, de Silva!' It was Sanjeewa. 'Forgive the delay. I would have called you before now, but I was waylaid by a guest, and it was hard to escape. I have the information you asked me for. Mr O'Halloran paid his bill by a cheque drawn on Haig and King's bank in Colombo.'

De Silva thanked him and made a call to the bank. Afterwards, he telephoned the Residence.

'What news?' asked Frobisher.

'I spoke to the bank manager. He agreed to keep my call confidential. Naturally, I didn't tell him exactly why I wanted to know about O'Halloran's account, but he assured me O'Halloran hasn't drawn any large sums of cash recently. Apparently, the account has never contained a lot of money in any case; neither has the bank made him any large loans.'

'I think we're onto something. I'm afraid I have bad news though. I've just met Florence Clutterbuck in the hall. She mentioned that O'Halloran and Laura Godley left earlier today. They were planning to go down to Colombo. He said he had business to attend to there.'

'Did he say how long they'd be away?'

'A few days. They only took a small amount of luggage.'

De Silva's brow furrowed. 'They may suspect we're onto them. If O'Halloran's behind Phoebe Tankerton's kidnapping, he might have a way of shipping out the ransom money through Colombo. I'll call the bank again and tell them to notify me straight away if he makes a deposit.' He paused. 'We'd better put a tail on him. No, on reflection, I think I'll go down myself. Do you know how he planned to travel?'

'Florence said they were taking the early afternoon train. I'll come with you. If we step on it, we should be in Kandy in time to meet it.'

Apprehensively, de Silva considered the prospect of the drive to Kandy with Charlie Frobisher in his MG and found it alarming. In any case, he had his own men to think of. He'd need Nadar to stay in Nuala to keep an eye on Johannes, but it would be unfair to Prasanna to cut him out of the action.

'I'm grateful for the offer, but I think my sergeant will be useful to us. I'll drive him down in my own car.'

'Righto. I'll have a word with the boss straight away. I reckon he'll be persuaded this is worth a shot. All being well, I'll be with you shortly.'

* * *

Keeping up with the scarlet MG proved hair-raising at times, but de Silva was pleased to find that the Morris acquitted herself well. They left behind the undulating green landscape of the Hill Country and descended into the plains where rice paddies and farms of rubber and banana trees sparkled in the sunshine. Apart from bullock and handcarts loaded with produce, there was little other traffic on the road. To de Silva's relief, Frobisher managed to avoid colliding with anything.

Slowly acclimatising himself to Frobisher's style of driving, de Silva had to admit that it was exhilarating: the wind in one's face and the scenery on either side of the road streaming past like a reel of film on fast forward.

It was dark by the time they reached the busy streets of Kandy and had to slow down. The last lap to the station was an anxious time, but despite the delays they encountered, they arrived just before the train was due. De Silva and Frobisher found the station master and explained that the Hill Country train would have to be held at Kandy while they searched it and no passengers allowed to get off until they gave the all clear. Ideally, passengers should remain in their compartments.

The station master looked unhappy. 'The passengers will not like it,' he said, waggling his head.

'That can't be helped,' said de Silva. 'This is a matter of great importance.' He hoped that if the man resisted, it would be possible to contact William Petrie for support, but luckily, after some puffing and blowing, the station master capitulated, and it wasn't necessary.

When the train finally came into sight, trundling slowly down the last stretch of track before it pulled up alongside the platform, de Silva delegated Prasanna to wait at the exit barrier while he and Frobisher prepared to search.

They began with First Class, starting one at either end to check in every carriage, but at first, all they encountered were curious looks and impatient glares. Some passengers came out into the corridor to find out what was causing the delay. One of them, a Britisher with the air of someone who wasn't used to being thwarted, buttonholed de Silva. 'What's the meaning of this?' he asked irritably. 'I have important business in town, and I haven't time to waste.'

Biting his tongue, de Silva suppressed the thought that

if he had been a British officer, the man would not have behaved so rudely. He needed to get on with the job in hand, however, so he answered with civility. Muttering, the man returned to his compartment.

Suddenly, he heard his name being called and saw Frobisher beckoning to him from the other end of the corridor of the section he was searching. De Silva hurried to join him.

'I've found O'Halloran,' Frobisher said in a low voice.

'Is one of the guards keeping an eye on him for us?'

Frobisher shook his head. 'No need for that, I'm afraid. He's dead as a doornail. You'd better come and see.'

* * *

O'Halloran lay on the floor of the carriage between the leather-covered benches on either side. His back was arched, and his torso sharply twisted at the waist, so that he was only partly in contact with the floor. One arm was flung out to the side, the hand clawing at a seat, as if he had been trying to pull himself up. His eyes were open, and his face was set in a grotesque, contorted expression, his tongue lolling from the side of his mouth.

The ugly sight was at odds with the elegance of the carriage's pretty etched-glass lamps and the colourful railway posters advertising the delights that awaited travellers in Ceylon. Delights O'Halloran was beyond enjoying now. Whatever his crimes, de Silva felt a pang of pity for him. He must have died in agony.

'When I found him, the curtains were drawn on the inside of the compartment,' said Frobisher. 'I thought I'd better leave them that way.'

'A wise decision. We don't want onlookers.'

'The body's still warm,' Frobisher went on. 'He can't

have been dead long. No wounds or contusions that I can see. It looks like he was poisoned.'

Remembering a case from years ago when he was still on the force in Colombo, de Silva nodded. 'With strychnine, I'd say, although we'll need a medical examination to tell us for sure. It causes violent convulsions and is very quick to take effect.'

He bent down and picked up a handkerchief that was half hidden under one of the seats. The scent of expensive perfume met his nostrils. 'Either the cleaners haven't been doing their job properly, or there was a lady in here with him. I think we can assume she was Laura Godley.'

Frobisher nodded.

'Have you spoken to the guard for this part of the train?' asked de Silva.

'Not yet, but now you're here, I'll go and find him.'

He returned a few moments later. 'The guard says there was a lady in the compartment with O'Halloran. Tall with dark hair, and well dressed.'

'Hmm. As we thought. Otherwise known as Mrs O'Halloran, if Aldous Barnett's telling us the truth. As long as the guards are following instructions and not letting anyone off the train, she can't have gone far.'

'Shall I get one of them to stay with the body while you and I look for her?' asked Frobisher. 'I presume she'll have stayed in First Class. She'd be pretty conspicuous anywhere else.'

De Silva nodded. 'I'll wait while you fetch one.'

When the guard arrived, he took one look at O'Halloran's body and backed gingerly towards the door of the compartment. 'You wanted me, sahib?' he asked de Silva.

'No need to be alarmed, man. He's not going to bite you. I just need you to keep an eye on him while Mr Frobisher and I search the rest of the train. Whoever killed him must be here somewhere.'

The look of anxiety on the guard's face changed to horror. De Silva drew in a deep breath then expelled it sharply. He pointed to the short stick hanging from the guard's belt. 'I very much doubt you'll need to defend yourself. Our victim won't be any use now to whoever killed him, so I doubt they'll want to come back here, but if they do, you've got that to protect you.'

'Yes, sahib,' the guard said unhappily.

On the way down the train, irate passengers who had ignored the instructions to stay in their compartments kept getting in the way, but slowly, de Silva and Frobisher eliminated the remaining carriages in First Class. Still there was no sign of Laura Godley.

'Do you think it's possible she's changed her clothes?' asked Frobisher. 'She might have moved to Second or even Third Class if she had something to wear that wouldn't draw attention to herself.'

'I think it's very possible,' said de Silva grimly. Laura Godley was a clever woman. It would be hard to find her in the crowded compartments of Second and Third Class. 'I'll make sure the guard knows he mustn't leave his post then we'd better get on with it.'

He was returning to the compartment where O'Halloran lay when there was the sound of hooting and another train pulled in at the opposite platform. A moment later, the doors started to bang open, disgorging the passengers. As they flooded out, the platform became a noisy sea of men, women, children, and even a few goats. Bags, bundles, and battered suitcases were shouldered; ancient bicycles wheeled, and errant children shouted after. De Silva's heart sank. If Laura Godley managed to get off their train, she might easily lose herself in the mêlée.

Back in the compartment where he had left O'Halloran and the guard, he went to the window and leaned out. Hard as he tried to peer through the crowds, it was impossible to see Sergeant Prasanna. The best course of action now would be to find him and together watch the passengers as they went through the exit barrier. It might be a forlorn hope that they would spot Laura Godley if she tried to make her escape, but all they could do was try.

Pushing his way through the crowd, he looked to left and right but didn't recognise any of the faces. Of course, many of the women were veiled; that would make it very difficult to recognise Godley if she was among them. He was resigning himself to the strong possibility that they had lost her when he saw Sergeant Prasanna by the barrier. In one hand he was clutching a large briefcase and handcuffed to the other was a woman in a black burka: Laura Godley.

CHAPTER 32

Much as de Silva liked and admired Charlie Frobisher, he was delighted that it was one of his own men who had not only caught Laura Godley, but also recovered the Tankerton ransom. Sergeant Prasanna was like a dog with two tails. De Silva hoped that Nadar's nose was not going to be out of joint.

'How clever of Sergeant Prasanna to spot her,' said Jane when he telephoned late that night to tell her the news and reassure her that he was safe and sound. 'Especially with all those people around her.'

'It was the shoes,' said de Silva. 'Third Class passengers would go barefoot or wear rope sandals. As Laura Godley was getting close to the barrier, he noticed that she wore good shoes.'

'Most observant of him. And the briefcase?'

'That, she was carrying under the burka. As for the ransom to be paid for Marie's release, Haig and King's Bank has confirmed that Hank O'Halloran never withdrew the money.'

'I wonder what was really in the bag.'

'Old newspapers maybe; or something along those lines. He must have been confident none of us would ask to look inside. In the same vein, I think we can safely assume the threatening letters he claimed to have received in India never existed.'

'I see. Do you know how O'Halloran was poisoned?'

'Laura Godley had an empty hip flask in her possession that smelt of brandy. If I'm right about the poison being strychnine, I think it must have been in that. Strychnine is relatively easy to obtain in small quantities, as it's used in a variety of Indian medicinal tonics, but more usefully from a poisoner's point of view, the British pharmacies over here often sell larger quantities for use as a pesticide.'

'But doesn't it have a very bitter taste? I'm sure I remember reading that somewhere. Surely, Hank O'Halloran would have noticed and been suspicious after his first mouthful, and would one be enough? He might have spat it out.'

'It's a good point, but David Hebden has a theory that may explain what happened. You're right that strychnine is a poison that's hard to get a victim to swallow, even in a strongly flavoured drink. But if it's mixed with potassium bromide, the bromide acts as a precipitant and sends the strychnine granules to the bottom of the liquid. If Laura Godley was careful not to shake the flask after she added the strychnine, she could even have risked a small sip herself to put O'Halloran off the scent. His first swig would probably have tasted no different from unadulterated brandy. Of course, by the time he came to drain the flask, the taste would have been very bitter—'

'But by then,' interposed Jane, 'his taste buds would have been less acute due to the effect of the brandy.'

'Exactly. Potassium bromide is easier to obtain than strychnine,' he went on. 'I've given Prasanna and Nadar the job of going around to all the pharmacies and Indian medical centres in Nuala, armed with a description of Laura Godley. If someone confirms that she bought either or both items from them, it will be powerful evidence against her.'

'I wonder how she would have had all that medical knowledge,' mused Jane. 'And why would she want him dead? You said that when you spoke to her at the Crown, she seemed almost to hero worship him, and she seemed genuinely distressed by Marie's death.'

'That's certainly the impression she gave, but who knows what was going on underneath. It may all have been an act. It's possible she was his wife and not his secretary.'

'So, do you believe that Marie was not their daughter?' she asked after he had told her Aldous Barnett's story.

'I'm not sure yet. There's a lot I still need to find out.'

'What's been done with Laura Godley, and O'Halloran's body?'

'Both down in Kandy. William Petrie made the arrangements for everything to be handled with discretion. He didn't want the Tankertons subjected to more distress.'

'How like him to be so thoughtful. I'm sure if the news got out, there would be quite a scandal, and it would be hard to keep their names out of it. I know it's been a horrible experience for Phoebe,' she went on. 'But in a strange way, this whole business may have done her and her parents some good. Florence was saying it seems to have brought them together. All the same, I'm sure they'll be very sad to know that O'Halloran was the villain of the piece rather than the friend he professed to be.'

'Angry too, I imagine.'

'I'm sure. When are you coming home?'

He yawned. 'Soon, I hope, but right now, I need a good sleep. I'm sorry if I woke you.'

'I wasn't asleep, but now I know you're alright, I will be very soon.'

'I'm sorry I didn't call sooner.'

'I understand. Sleep well, dear.'

'You too, my love.'

CHAPTER 33

A few days later.

With a small pile of books to return tucked under her arm, Jane was going into the library when she met Emerald on her way out.

'Jane! How nice to see you!' Emerald took one of the books she had just borrowed from her bag. 'Look, a detective story! You've infected me with your taste. I used to read nothing but romances.' She lowered her voice. 'I was planning to come and see you anyway. Is there any news about Laura Godley, and is it really true she was Hank O'Halloran's wife?'

'Shanti thinks it may be true, but we'd better move away from here before I tell you more.'

They went to sit on a bench in the small patch of garden to one side of the library building.

'I expect you know that your clever husband came up with the solution as to how she would have made O'Halloran take the strychnine without him noticing its bitter taste,' said Jane.

Emerald smiled. 'Yes. He said it was the kind of thing any doctor would know, but I told him not to be so modest.'

'I'm still puzzled though about how Laura Godley knew it, but perhaps Shanti will find out. In any case, he gave Sergeant Prasanna and Constable Nadar the job of going around all the medical centres and pharmacies in Nuala with a description of Laura Godley, and if she'd shopped at any of them, finding out what she bought. It turns out that a woman who gave a different name but matched her description bought strychnine from one of the pharmacies. It wasn't the first time she'd been in, but they weren't suspicious because she said she needed the poison to kill rats in the place where she was living.'

'What about the other things?'

'She may have already had a supply of the chloroform used on Phoebe, if that's what it was. As for the potassium bromide, she bought that from another pharmacy. To get it, she claimed to suffer from seizures and said she needed it to control them. The pharmacist thought it was odd at the time, because potassium bromide is a rather old-fashioned medication, but Godley insisted she had always taken it and wanted to continue. She showed him a doctor's letter.'

'From a doctor in Nuala?'

Jane shook her head. 'Shanti was pleased that Prasanna and Nadar thought to check that. No, it wasn't. The letter-heading was for a doctor in Calcutta, but of course it might have been a forgery.'

'It's still all very mysterious,' said Emerald. 'If Godley and O'Halloran hatched the plan to get the ransom money out of the Tankertons together, why do you think she wanted him dead? And where did Marie O'Halloran fit in?'

'She may not have been O'Halloran's daughter, but I hope Shanti will have more to say about that when he comes home. He's still down at the police station in Kandy, questioning Laura Godley. I'm not expecting him back until tomorrow. Very kindly, Lady Caroline Petrie has been putting him up at the Petries' official residence.'

'David's out this evening as well.'

'Then why don't you come and have supper at Sunnybank? It would be lovely to have the company.'

'I'd be delighted. I have the car, so if you like, I can drive you home.'

'That would be nice. With Shanti away, I'm having to travel by rickshaw unless kind friends help me out. Give me a moment to return these books and then I'll be ready.'

* * *

Back at Sunnybank, the late afternoon sun slanted across the garden, but the air was still warm. Jane and Emerald sat on the verandah sipping cooling drinks while they chatted. Emerald was in mid-sentence when she was interrupted by a plaintive meow. She stopped and looked down then smiled. 'I didn't know you and Shanti had a kitten. When did you get it?'

'Actually, there are two of them,' said Jane. 'I think they must be orphans. They've been coming to be fed for a while now. Shanti doesn't know about them yet. What with the case keeping him so busy, he's not had much time at home. I hope he won't mind.'

A second black kitten detached itself from the shadows, while the one that had arrived first padded over to Emerald and rubbed up against her leg. She bent down to stroke it. 'What a dear little thing, and quite bold.'

'The little girl is shyer,' said Jane. She put out her hand and the other kitten came to her but kept a wary eye on Emerald.

'You'll have to keep them, you know,' Emerald said with a laugh. 'Once an animal decides to adopt you, that's final.'

'I'd love to. I've always been fond of cats, but Shanti might not be so keen.'

'Surely he will. He's talked to me about the pets he had as a child and obviously loved them.'

'Yes, a bird and a mongoose.'

'It will be a nice surprise for him when he comes home. Have you decided what to call them yet?' Emerald lifted the boy kitten and held him up in front of her. Paws dangling, he gazed at her calmly. 'He reminds me of a cat we had at home in Ireland. He was called Billy.'

Jane thought for a moment. 'I like that.' She picked up the little girl and put her in her lap. 'And you can be Bella.'

She reached for the bell on the table at her side. 'I'm sure they're both hungry. I'll tell one of the servants to bring their supper.'

CHAPTER 34

'I'll have to go back to Kandy again in a day or two,' said de Silva. 'But welcoming as the Petries have been, I'm very glad to be home.'

He rubbed a hand over his face and stifled a yawn. It had been a long day.

'If you're too tired,' said Jane, 'tell me everything in the morning.'

He shook his head and smiled. 'Our good Hill Country air and this whisky,' he tapped a finger against the glass, 'and I'll be a new man.'

He took a sip. 'So, where shall I begin… Ah yes, William Petrie received the report on O'Halloran that he asked for from Scotland Yard – they moved a bit faster for him than they did for Archie with his request for information on Patterson. It turns out Hank O'Halloran and his wife, whom we now know posed here in Ceylon as his secretary, Laura Godley, were confidence tricksters. The British police have been trying to track them down for some time, but they gave them the slip and left England to go travelling. They ended up in India, which is where, as you told me, they met the Tankertons. O'Halloran wasn't Hank's real name; he was born Henry Hart, but he also went by the name of Harlan.'

Jane's brow furrowed. 'I still don't understand where Marie fitted in.'

'I'll come to that. O'Halloran, or rather Hart, lied about being born in America. He was born in England but went to America in his twenties hoping to make a career in acting. For a few years, he played minor parts in Hollywood films using his real name, but when his career slumped, he had to rely on a succession of badly paid jobs. As we know from Aldous Barnett, he tried to make more money out of insurance fraud. When he realised that he was in danger of being exposed and arrested, he left for England.'

Jane stood up and went to her bureau, opened it and brought out a magazine. 'I was going to throw this out with the others, but in the end, I kept it to show you.' She put the magazine in his lap.

'What am I supposed to be looking at?'

Jane pointed. 'This photograph.'

De Silva peered at it. 'Isn't that the actor you're so keen on? What's his name?'

'Cary Grant. But it's the man three places to his left I want you to look at. I was sure there was something familiar about him, but I couldn't put my finger on what it was.'

Briefly, de Silva studied the photograph. 'I suppose it might be O'Halloran as a young man. Is that what you mean?'

'Yes, and I wish I'd realised sooner why I recognised him.'

De Silva smiled. 'Even you are not perfect, my love.'

She glowered at him then laughed.

'I'm intrigued to know how Laura Godley knew so much about the use of strychnine,' she went on.

'Before she met and married O'Halloran in England – she is British by the way, the American accent was part of the disguise, as was O'Halloran's – she was a nurse. She'd ended up working privately for a wealthy elderly man who needed full-time care. He died very suddenly, and because of his age and infirmity, no one was suspicious, but in the light of what's happened, I can't help thinking that he might have been Godley's first victim.'

'Has she confessed to killing O'Halloran?'

'Yes, and she's been charged with Romesh's murder. O'Halloran didn't have the opportunity to go alone to Romesh's house after Phoebe was kidnapped, but Laura did. Both she and O'Halloran had good reason for wanting Romesh dead. As your British saying goes, dead men tell no tales. There's also the evidence of the boy Sergeant Prasanna found. The burka he described the lady he saw wearing matched what Godley wore when she was apprehended at Kandy station.'

'You still haven't told me how Marie fitted into all this, and who killed her and why. Or why Laura wanted O'Halloran dead.'

De Silva took another sip of his whisky. 'As to why Laura wanted O'Halloran dead, it was because of Marie. She wasn't O'Halloran's daughter, just an aspiring actress he and Laura had picked up in London to play that part before they left the country to try their luck abroad. They reckoned that it would be a clever move to travel as a businessman with his secretary and daughter rather than alone as husband and wife. Laura chose the name Godley rather than using her maiden name which was Garvey.

'She'd known even before she married him that her husband was often unfaithful. She was prepared to turn a blind eye to the clandestine affair she was sure he and Marie soon embarked on. That was until she overheard them talking together when they thought they were alone. Marie claimed she was pregnant with O'Halloran's child, and she wanted him to leave Laura.'

'Gosh! Do you think Marie was telling the truth?'

'Impossible to know, and it's too late to examine the body now. The crucial point is that true or not, Laura Godley decided that she'd had enough. O'Halloran had never treated her well. Quite apart from his unfaithfulness, he liked to gamble. Often, he lost his share of any money that they made, and she had to bail him out. She was used to that, but the thought of Marie having his baby was too much for her. She'd always longed for a baby and had never been able to have one.'

'Was it O'Halloran's idea to murder Marie, or did he and Laura plan it together?'

'It may have been O'Halloran's idea originally, in order to be rid of a lover who had become troublesome, but Laura doesn't appear to have tried to dissuade him. Of course, he didn't mention the baby to Laura, just that Marie was getting greedy and wanting more money, so it was time she was discarded. When they arrived in Nuala, Laura found the house in Ridgeway Road and engaged the services of Johannes and Romesh to help her set up the séance room and carry out the actual kidnap. Laura also prepared herself to pose as the medium.'

Jane rested her chin on her cupped hand. 'I suppose it would have been easy enough for her to come and go from the Crown as she pleased,' she said.

'Yes. O'Halloran had very conveniently said he had no need of her services while he and Marie were at the Residence. The story he told Marie was that his plan was for both her and Phoebe to be kidnapped at the party at the Residence. Phoebe would be exchanged for real money, and Marie for a bogus ransom. After the ransoms were paid, and she and Phoebe were handed back, Marie would tell a heartrending, but untrue, story of how frightened she'd been, kept separated from Phoebe in a damp, dirty cellar where she thought she would never be found. She would say that she'd been terrified of starving to death or being killed by the kidnappers if they thought either of the girls' fathers was trying to trick them. Phoebe would no doubt give a supporting account of her own, actual, experience. To add to the drama Marie would say that one evening she had heard a voice in the corridor that sounded like Patterson's. The intention was to lead us to suspect him, as of course, for a long time, we did.'

'I suppose Marie's acting skills would have been an asset.'

'I imagine so. She may not have been a great actress, but I'm sure charm would have served her well.'

He paused for a moment. 'Where was I? Ah, yes. When, on O'Halloran's secret orders, Romesh and Johannes took only Marie, O'Halloran got a message to her via Laura that his men had bungled their task and he was furious with them. He claimed he might have to abandon the whole plan to kidnap Phoebe, but he wasn't giving up yet. He needed to maintain the fiction that Marie really had been kidnapped, so the handover must proceed as planned. We'll never know if Marie believed him and whether she was being held prisoner or not.'

Jane sighed. 'I know that in the circumstances, it's hard to feel much sympathy for Marie, but it's sad to think that she paid such a terrible price for her misdeeds. As for Laura, what a dreadful situation to find herself in. After everything she'd already put up with, it's no wonder she turned against O'Halloran. But if she helped him with Marie's murder, killed Romesh to silence him, and possibly murdered the old gentlemen she was looking after as a nurse, it's very hard to have any sympathy for her.'

'Indeed. She wasn't there when Marie was killed, so we're not sure exactly how the scene played out, but I'm fairly sure it was O'Halloran, not Romesh or Johannes, who pulled the trigger. He might then have got rid of the gun at the scene of the crime. I regret that we never searched the whole area properly. We were too busy with O'Halloran and then following the kidnappers in the direction he indicated. Alternatively, he may have concealed it on his person and disposed of it later. He could have given it to Laura when she visited him at the Residence.'

'Do you think that Romesh and Johannes knew in advance, or actually witnessed, the murder?'

'I'm not sure. Either or both of them could have been instructed to leave immediately after delivering her to the clearing. Johannes will have to be interrogated on that issue, but he may well deny knowing Marie was to be killed or claim still not to know that she had been. It's not that easy getting much sense out of him. One thing's for sure, he was lucky, or unusually clever, when he decided to disappear after Phoebe was kidnapped, or he might have ended up dead like his friend Romesh.'

'What will happen to Johannes?' asked Jane, an expression of slight concern on her face.

'Despite the temptation to feel sorry for him, we know him to have participated in two kidnaps, and he may have had a conscious role in delivering Marie to her death, so he might be held responsible as an accessory to her murder. Archie and William Petrie agree we can speak up for him in terms of his poor reasoning ability, but he must stand trial.'

Before continuing, de Silva went to the decanter on the sideboard and poured himself another small tot of whisky. He felt he deserved it.

'Of course, with Marie dead, an important part of the plot to implicate Patterson – Marie alleging she heard him talking to the kidnappers – was lost, so O'Halloran came up with the idea of planting Patterson's business card at the scene of Marie's murder. While they were travelling, Patterson had handed out cards whenever he came across a potential future client. O'Halloran had no difficulty getting hold of one.'

'So Patterson is completely in the clear?'

'Yes.'

De Silva stopped, staring at something at the far end of the verandah. 'What on earth is that?'

Billy, the kitten, jumped onto the top of the railing and confidently picked his way along to the place where it ended by the top of the garden steps. With one paw, he started to bat at a large moth that had flown in from the rapidly darkening garden, attracted by the light of a nearby lamp.

'I've been meaning to tell you, but there's been so much going on.' Jane paused as Bella appeared from behind de Silva's chair, regarded him thoughtfully for a moment then jumped onto his lap.

Jane beamed. 'See, she likes you, and she's been so shy up until now.'

Frowning, de Silva looked down at the kitten, and for a moment, Jane's confidence ebbed.

'You won't mind if we keep them, will you, dear?' she asked tentatively. 'Emerald and I think they must have lost their mother. She suggested Billy as a nice name for the little boy, and I like Bella for the little girl.'

'So, I am outvoted, is that it?' asked de Silva, doing his best to look stern.

'Of course not.'

He watched as Billy lost interest in the moth, yawned, and curled up at the top of the steps to the garden. Bella remained in his lap. So, this explained the damage in the garden shed and to his vegetable patch, as well as the mysterious shadows on the drive. The pair of them certainly seemed to be at home. Who was he to spoil it for them, or for Jane?

In the last few days, three lives had ended. If Marie O'Halloran was to be believed, a fourth had also been snuffed out when it had hardly begun. It was a propitious time to find space in their own lives to help two new ones.

He chuckled. 'If it pleases you, my love, we'll keep them, and I'm happy to defer to you and Emerald in the choice of names.'

Leaning across, Jane kissed his cheek. 'Thank you, my dear. I'm sure you won't regret it.'

Made in the USA
Middletown, DE
20 April 2021